Kill Switch

A Kyle Callahan Mystery

Mark McNease

Also By Mark McNease

Audiobooks
A House in the Woods
Black Cat White Paws
Murder at Pride Lodge
Pride and Perilous
Death by Pride
Death in the Headlights
Last Room at the Cliff's Edge
Stop the Car

Mysteries and Thrillers
A House in the Woods
Black Cat White Paws
Murder at Pride Lodge
Pride and Perilous
Death in the Headlights
Death by Pride
Kill Switch
Last Room at the Cliff's Edge

Other Books and Writing
Stop the Car: A Kindle Single
The Seer: A Short Story
Rough & Tumble: A Dystopian Love Tragedy
An Unobstructed View: Short Fiction
5 of a Kind: More Short Fiction

Visit Mark McNease.com
Join the author's mailing list for updates

Acknowledgments

It's time I acknowledge my very own "beta reader" and husband Frank Murray, who reads each one of these mysteries. He highlights, underlines, and questions why I write things a certain way, then asks if I meant *this* when I wrote *that* (in addition to pointing out the misspellings). It's a lot to ask of someone and to know he'll do it, not because he has to, but because we're in this messy thing called life together.

Also a big thanks to my copy editor-slash-proofreader Robin Feldman. Not only does she catch the big and small stuff, but she questions my colloquialisms.

And, after five Kyle Callahan Mysteries, I must thank the fans of the series. I should have done that after the first book. You know who you are: You write me emails telling me how much you enjoyed the newest book and you make me want to write another.

Thank you, thank you.

- Mark McNease

For Edwin James Berry
Did you think I'd forgotten?

And for Bob Delegall
I miss the laughter most.

Part I

Among the Living

CHAPTER One

Kyle Callahan glanced around his therapist's office. He'd sat in this overstuffed beige leather chair, talking to this gentle and soft-spoken man for the past six months, and still there were small details he would notice on a visit that he hadn't seen before. A photograph of Peter Benoit's daughter, now in her second year at Princeton. A small, cheap plaster bust of Chopin, Peter's favorite composer, staring blindly from the bookshelf. A book about circuses among the dozens on psychology, psychiatry, and the byzantine workings of the human mind. And tonight: a set of bronzed baby shoes on Peter's desk. Kyle never sat at or beside the desk. He only looked at it tucked tightly into a corner of the room beneath a window with a view of Columbus Avenue. It was as mysterious as his therapist—he only knew about the daughter and the love for Chopin by asking questions, a reversal of roles that had happened perhaps a half dozen times over the course of twenty-four one hour sessions spent talking about his life since the killing. Correction, the shooting, as Peter reminded him. Yes, Kyle had killed a man. Yes, it had been In self-defense. Yes, it had ended the nightmarish career of the Pride Killer, among New York City's most successful and cruel sociopaths. So, rightly, Peter Benoit (pronounced "Ben-wah") reminded Kyle from time to time that it was not murder. But that didn't change how Kyle felt. It didn't erase his guilt, however unnecessary. He had taken a man's life in an Upper East Side townhouse basement, and he had been trying to live with it ever since.

"I haven't seen bronzed baby shoes since I was a kid," Kyle said, looking at the desk. "I started to ask if they still made them, but obviously those were made a long time ago. Are they yours?"

"Yes, Kyle, they're mine," Peter responded. "I was that small once. We all were."

"Are they really bronze?"

"I don't know. My mother had them made. But they look bronze."

"Yes, they do."

Kyle turned his attention back to Peter. Lately he'd found himself attracted to the therapist and it made him uncomfortable. He knew it wasn't real—not *real* real—and that it was some kind of "transference," but it made him uneasy. It didn't help that the therapist was quite tall and handsome, late-forties, with brown hair shot through with gray; blue eyes, large hands, and much too relaxed for anyone living and working in New York City.

"What were we talking about?" Kyle asked, trying to refocus.

"Your father's death," said Peter.

"Really?"

"Yes, Kyle. You were visiting your parents in Highland Park. You went in to see your father in his study and you found him slumped over his desk—the same desk you now have in your spare room at home."

Kyle thought about it. He could not understand how talking about killing Diedrich Kristof Keller III—the Pride Killer—had morphed into talking about his dead father. Or how it led to talking about his relationship with his husband, Danny. Or his job. Or anything, really. None of those things were why he'd come here, but they had entered his conversations with his therapist and he was as uncomfortable with that as he was with feeling attracted to the man. Psychoanalysis was a curious, dangerous beast, and Kyle wasn't sure he'd made the right decision letting it out of its cage.

"He didn't like me," Kyle said. Just like that. Flat, true.

"What made you think that?"

"You don't believe me?"

"I didn't say that. I just asked why you thought your father didn't like you."

Kyle stared at him. "Because he told me."

There, it had happened again. Another unsettling truth uttered as if he'd said it was cold in the room or that he'd left his umbrella at home and it was raining. This had happened quite a few times over the months. Bits and pieces of memories, emotions and unpleasant realities popping out into the air, floating there for a moment, then falling to the floor or staining his heart.

"How did it happen?" Peter asked.

"How did what happen?"

"How did your father tell you he didn't like you? Were you having an argument? Was it a response to something that had been said?"

Kyle remembered it clearly now, just like he remembered finding his father dead at his desk—a not-so-repressed memory he'd told very few people. His mother knew; she was in the house that day, too. Danny, of course. But almost no one else.

Kyle had been at the kitchen table having breakfast. He was twenty at the time. Twenty-one? He was in love with David Grogan, the young man he pursued to New York City from Chicago where they'd both attended college. He'd made the decision to move but not yet done it. His father had not taken kindly to Kyle's being gay. It wasn't rejection, per se, but more of a further distancing to an already distant relationship. Kyle's father had taken the news coolly, as he'd taken all of Kyle's decisions in life. As if he didn't care.

"I told him I was moving to New York," Kyle said, recalling it now in the therapist's office. "He shrugged. He said, 'Fine,' or something like that. Something short and disinterested. 'Don't you care?' I asked him. I didn't want him to oppose the move—I was hell bent, as my mother said, on chasing David across the country—but *something*."

"You wanted him to take it as a loss," Peter said.

"Yes, yes, I did."

"But that's not what happened."

"Not at all," Kyle said. He looked down now, worried his eyes might water. "I said, 'That's all you have to say? 'Fine?' And he just ... I don't know ... took a bite of his toast, looked at me and said, 'I don't like you, Kyle.'"

"It must have hurt."

Kyle felt his facial muscles tighten. He hated being told such clear simple truths. Of course it hurt. And of course Kyle had never told anyone before tonight what his father had said, or how deeply it cut him.

"Yes," Kyle said. "It hurt. Then he got up and went to his study. To his desk. Where I found him dead twenty-five years later. Can we change the subject?"

Peter was sensitive, which was not surprising. He was a very experienced therapist and knew when to let things rest. He paused for a moment to drink some of the ginger tea he always had on the stand beside his chair. Kyle knew it was a way of shifting away from one subject to another. Peter Benoit was not the only one in the room who could read people.

"How are the nightmares?" Peter asked, setting his teacup back down.

It was a question the therapist hadn't asked for several weeks. Kyle was glad of the omission; he preferred not to talk about the dreams that had plagued him since the shooting in Diedrich Keller's basement. They'd stopped for a while—a short while—but had returned the last week, as distressing as ever. The dreams' scenario changed slightly, their sequence of events, but they always ended the same: with Kyle sobbing over the body of the serial killer he'd just stopped with a bullet to the heart, while his husband Danny and his friend Detective Linda Sikorsky lay dead at the hands of the man he'd murdered.

"It wasn't murder," Peter said the first time Kyle described the dreams. "It was kill or be killed. You need to remember that."

Kill or be killed. A struggle, a twist of fate, a gunshot, and Kyle had taken a life. He knew it should matter whose life he had taken — a brutal killer who had claimed fourteen victims over seven years and who'd been within a knife blade's distance from killing Danny — but watching a man die at your own hand defied emotional logic. Death was death. And as he'd seen the life quickly flee from Diedrich Keller's eyes, he'd felt as if he had been tattooed forever by it. Then the dreams began and he sought out a therapist to try and stop them.

"Not so bad, or so often," Kyle lied. He'd had a dream just the night before.

"Good," said Peter, doubting Kyle had told him the truth. "How about your photography?"

Kyle looked up at him. Once upon a time, not long ago, he'd been an avid amateur photographer. The passion had lasted about fifteen years, ever since his father had given him an expensive camera for his fortieth birthday. Then the murders at Pride Lodge, Kyle standing over the empty blue pool taking photographs of his friend Teddy's broken body at the bottom; his first and only photo exhibit at the Katherine Pride Gallery, just days after the madman Kieran Stipling had been stopped from cutting Stuart Pride's throat. It was all connected, Kyle knew. The murders, the murderers, and his photography. As one entered his life, the other left. Now he no longer took pictures and had no desire to.

"It's still on hold," Kyle said, knowing it would probably stay there. Maybe he would someday see something he thought would look amazing through a camera lens, or a face that needed preserving in a photograph, or a scene. But not anytime soon. His camera had lain on a shelf in the spare room gathering dust for six months.

Peter leaned forward. It was usually a signal their fifty minutes were coming to a close.

"Have you given some thought to what I suggested?" Peter asked.

The therapist had been encouraging Kyle to take on something new — another passion, another pastime. Kyle had expressed for the first time his interest in getting into the reporting end of his career. If his boss Imogene could do it, he could, too. He'd even begun contributing to her stories — uncredited, of course. He was writing copy now, under Imogene's tutelage. He knew he was too old to become a reporter, but there may be ways to contribute. No one knew what editors looked like, and Kyle had discovered he had a knack for writing and editing as well as being the best personal assistant Imogene had ever had. He was good for more than bagels and coffee and answering her emails well past quitting time.

"Yes, I have thought about it," Kyle said. "And Imogene thinks it's a great idea. I've been working on stories with her. She's very experienced, she's teaching me a lot — about angles to stories and how to shape them."

"Good, good. And did you still want to try another anti-depressant?"

"Oh, God no!" Kyle said, as if he'd just tasted something bitter. "That was, like, a month ago when the nightmares were still a problem. Psychopharmacology is not for me."

He'd tried three different anti-depressants and each made him feel disembodied. No matter how low the dose, whatever they did to him was pronounced and unpleasant. He was glad to find a therapist who preferred talk to medication. Kyle had thrown the pills out each time and was now determined to find another way to deal with his . . . trauma. He didn't like the word. He didn't like thinking he'd been traumatized. But sometimes there was no better way to describe it.

What he did not tell Peter Benoit that night was that he'd been thinking through the suggestion to find a new interest and had come up with something very different from writing, editing or reporting. Something he was not ready to tell Peter about. Something that already had him waking up feeling better, clearer, and once again energized.

"Our time's up," Peter said gently. He always ended the sessions with his kind voice. Then, as he did from time to time, he said, "I'll be away next week." He reached for the Day Planner he kept next to his ginger tea, opened it and said, "Two weeks from tonight is okay for you?"

It was always okay for Kyle. Peter had only skipped three sessions in six months. He never said why; it was part of his mystique. Kyle knew his therapist was divorced—there were no photos of his ex-wife in the office. He knew he had a daughter, and a cat whose white hair was sometimes on the therapist's pants. But beyond that he knew very little.

"Two weeks is fine," Kyle said.

He stood up then and shook Peter's hand. He often wondered if they'd been at it long enough for a hug, but it was better to keep the distance.

"I'll see you in two weeks," said Kyle. He turned and let himself out of the office.

Tomorrow was Tuesday and he planned on working late with Imogene. The Manhattan District Attorney was under investigation for corruption and it was a huge story, with developments breaking daily. He would be in the office well into the evening.

He would also be paying a visit to someone who could help him find his new obsession, his path back to the life he'd known.

CHAPTER Two

Raul Sandoval was the first Latino to be elected District Attorney for Manhattan in the city's history. It had been a big deal the first time he won office, and solidified as historic with his reelection. No one could say it was a fluke, or the outcome of an electorate eager to prove its progressive credentials, or simply an act of bad judgment on the part of voters. He was popular, outspoken, preening, and currently under investigation for bribery. That was the story, as big now as his two elections had been. Four months into his second term, his anticipated fall made national news and had reporters for the city on death watch. Those reporters included Imogene Landis, English language correspondent for Tokyo Pulse, once an obscure and amusing woman to a 3:00 a.m. Tokyo crowd, now a star. She'd made the move from faltering, sometimes flailing financial reporter who knew neither Japanese nor much about Wall Street, to headliner for a growing foreign audience covering politics, scandal, culture, and anything else that might keep viewers glued to their television sets as Japanese sub-titles scrolled beneath her image. That change had come with her breathless coverage of the Pride Lodge murders over two years ago. It had reinvigorated her foundering career, made her a headliner for Japan TV3, producers of Tokyo Pulse, and resulted in several offers from stations around the United States, all of which Imogene had turned down. Perhaps she thought it was better to reign in Hell than serve in Heaven: she had no competition this way, and as long as she kept the stories coming she had a place to call her TV home.

Imogene was working late on the Sandoval story Tuesday night, which meant Kyle was working late with her. He'd been her assistant for seven years and had been grateful as well as surprised she had not taken a better deal in Seattle or

Phoenix or even Los Angeles. Not long ago he'd been certain she would leave and he would have to decide if being anyone's assistant was what he wanted to do in his late 50s, but the choice had not been forced on him and he was happy to leave it that way as long as possible.

Word among the newsies was that Sandoval was going to be indicted. Rumor had long speculated that he'd thrown cases, made back room agreements, and generally abused his power in exchange for large sums of cash. Imogene was running a series on the scandal for Tokyo Pulse and was working on a third update for the week. It was 8:00 p.m. when she noticed the clock and stood up from her desk, peering over the low partition that divided her cubicle from Kyle's (only the boss, Leonard "Lenny-san" Baumstein had an office).

"I'm hungry, Kyle," she said.

Kyle looked up at her from the script he'd been copyediting. Imogene was short and barely stood above the top of the partition. He'd seen her staring over at him a thousand times and it never ceased to amuse him. She didn't know this and never would — one did not risk offending Imogene, no matter how much one loved her or how deeply she returned the sentiment.

"Turkey and Swiss on a roll, toasted," Kyle said. "Two coffees."

"Make that four," she said. "I can see us here till midnight."

Kyle nodded, stood up and grabbed his windbreaker from the coat stand they shared. It was still chilly in late April. He said nothing more and hurried along the aisle, through the maze of cubicles in the newsroom and down the stairs to the street. The Japan TV3 offices were on the third floor, faster to reach by stair than by an elevator that was out of service half the time.

He'd been planning to go out anyway; it made it easier to have Imogene ask for food. This way he didn't need to take a break or explain where he was going — or why. He'd made his decision when he'd left Peter Benoit's office the night before, and he wasn't ready to discuss it with anyone. Not until he'd set things in motion. If he did what he'd decided to do, if he began examining pieces of this particular puzzle, he would have a talk with Danny in the morning to explain the what and why, then a Skype call with Detective Linda. He would need her as a sounding board, an objective adviser of sorts, if he was to make this sudden turn and head resolutely down this road. But first he had to pick up sandwiches.

The 38-Nine Deli was so named for being located at the corner of 38th Street and Ninth Avenue. It had stood there in continuous operation for forty years, though not run by the same operator. The 38-Nine, as everyone in the neighborhood called it, had changed hands several times. The older residents of Hell's Kitchen could remember a Jewish owner, a Korean owner, one gay couple who'd tried and failed to make the place upscale with imported teas and eco-friendly laundry detergent (they'd been the shortest-lived proprietors, lasting only six months) and now, for the past eight years, a Pakistani named Nizran Ramani. Everyone called him Niz. Sixty-two years old, five daughters no one ever saw and a wife, Meriem, who worked in the deli on weekends. Niz had managed to marry off three of his daughters but was still working on the other two. He wanted them out of the house but could not afford much in the way of a dowry.

Niz worked at the deli seven days a week. He could be seen at 6:00 a.m. opening the metal grate that slid across the storefront. By then the deli had been closed for two hours. That's the only amount of time in any twenty-four hour period Niz was willing to refuse customers. It was also when Skate Copley went home, locking the door and sliding the gate shut, securing the giant padlock when he left from his overnight shift.

Most people knew Skate's story. His birth name was Stuart Eldridge Copley. He'd been called Skate since his early teens, when he could be seen skateboarding around the streets and sidewalks of Sunnyside, Queens. The name stuck, and for most of his forty-seven years everyone called him Skate, with the exception of his parents and two sisters and his ex-wife Jennifer when she was angry with him. His paychecks still said Stuart, but he'd ignored the name so long he no longer saw it — they were just meaningless letters on paper.

Skate was not a name readily associated with a highly successful, intensely motivated financial manager, which is what Skate had been before his daughter's murder. He'd been many things before that night almost three years ago: wealthy, married, the owner of a 19th floor condo on Central Park South overlooking the Park. And most of all, most centrally to his life and its sudden crash, he'd been a father. A very doting, fretting, overly protective father who had, to his mind, failed spectacularly and permanently the one time it had mattered most. So for Skate it was a fair trade: everything his life had been, given as the price for his daughter. Everything he'd thought had meaning, exchanged for the only thing that did.

A man's fall from the heights can sometimes be nasty and public; Skate's had been both. A week after Corinne's murder he'd stopped answering calls from his office — Barton and Loman, one of the top financial firms in New York City, where Skate had worked his way up to number three. Before the murder he'd shifted millions of dollars of his clients' money from one fund to another, playing with portfolios with the skill of a man at the top of his game. After the murder no amount of money in the world, of his or anyone else's, could make the nightmare go away. Before the murder he'd been working on his marriage to Jennifer. It hadn't been on the rocks so much as weary after twenty years together. After the murder he had no interest in Jennifer, not her attempts to comfort him, not her ridiculous search for "closure," and not, a year later, her insistence that he move on from Corinne's death. He moved on, all right. On and out and down to Hell's Kitchen, two blocks from the scene of the crime. Out and away from Jennifer, who found her closure in another lawyer, moved to Boston, got remarried, and became the stepmother to a college boy. On and out of Barton and Loman, ignoring the pleas of old man Barton and the rest of them. Down and down and down some more, until now, for the past year and a half, he'd been working at the 38-Nine Deli, obsessed with someday, somehow, finding the man who took his daughter's life and ended his own in every meaningful way.

Niz knew the story. Niz took pity on Skate and hired him, specifically for the overnight shift Skate requested. He wanted to be there, in that environment, late at night. He wanted to watch the faces changes as night progressed. No baby strollers at midnight. No happy couples stopping in for a recipe ingredient they'd forgotten or a pint of ice cream at 1:00 a.m. Only denizens once the streets became ghostly and the sidewalks clicked beneath the feet of hustlers and whores and thieves. It was the thieves he was most interested in. One particular thief, who had stolen his daughter's phone.

She hadn't wanted to give it up. She'd resisted. Skate knew this because he'd been on the phone with her at that exact moment. She was going to dinner with friends. Skate was in his office; Corinne was on 37th Street walking west. Skate had told her many times to avoid the side streets. Being a seventeen-year-old, she had ignored him. He heard her speak to someone, then tell them to fuck off, language he never heard her use (well, almost never). Then he heard it: a loud pop. Nothing like the gunshots on TV.

"He wants my phone, Daddy," she'd said.

"Who, Baby? Who wants your phone?"

Then, "Fuck off!"

Then, the gunshot.

Then, everything changed. Skate was a new Skate. Skate began to live on hatred. Skate left behind all he'd known and traded it for the night watch and a shit apartment across from the Port Authority bus station.

Skate lived for the day he would stop waking up to the last words he'd said to his child.

"Speak to me! Baby, speak to me!"

Speak to me, jarring him from sleep night after night for three years. *Speak to me,* a never-ending echo from across a vast black canyon. They were the last words he spoke to her, his last plea.

She never responded.

Kyle knew Skate's story, too. He'd been seeing Skate at the deli on those nights he and Imogene worked late and he made a sandwich run. He didn't have all the details, only that the thin, pale man who worked the counter and cash register at the 38-Nine Deli had once been someone else, someone unrecognizable from the haunted ghost with a forced smile.

"How you doing tonight, Skate?" Kyle said.

He was alone in the deli. It was raining and the sidewalk traffic had dwindled as people without umbrellas hurried inside and the ones who had them kept moving, their heads down beneath covers of black fabric.

"Fine, Kyle."

Skate was always "fine."

Kyle ordered two turkey and Swiss sandwiches, Imogene's on a roll as requested with lettuce and tomato, his own on rye with a dollop of mayonnaise.

Kyle glanced around, looking to see if Niz was in. Sometimes the deli owner was there working on inventory or just wanting to get out of his house in Jackson Heights. He would step out from behind a row of canned goods, or come up from the basement, entering through the small back room just beyond the beer cooler. He did not appear to be there; nor was anyone else. No bored kids hanging out, no old people lingering at the cereal shelf.

"Listen, Skate ..." Kyle said, still trying to decide how to phrase his question.

"Yeah?" said Skate. He walked back the few steps from the counter where he made sandwiches and bagels, Kyle's order in his hand.

"I was wondering … about your daughter."

Skate Copley became still. He said nothing as he took a brown paper bag and placed the sandwiches in it. After a long moment, Kyle thought he'd made a mistake and that Skate was not going to answer him.

Skate finally looked up. "It'll be three years next week," he said. "April twenty-third."

"I know."

There had been a small item in the New York Times over the weekend. Corinne Copley's murder, the coldblooded shooting of her in what appeared to be a random robbery — the theft of her phone, the loss of her life for a handheld device — had made national news. If only she'd taken a different street. If only she'd arrived at that particular spot, at those particular coordinates in space and time, ten minutes later. If only she'd had a kill switch. The devices were more common now and allowed the owners of smartphones to nuke their phones if they were stolen or went missing, making them useless for thieves to sell on the black market. But she'd been there, just a block from where Kyle was buying his sandwiches. And her phone had not had a kill switch. By now it was most likely thrown out for a much newer model, or tossed aside in a drug den somewhere, or maybe still being used on a street corner in Hong Kong.

"Her murder was never solved," Kyle said. This was not new information to anyone who knew about the case.

"They tried," said Skate. "This detective from the Midtown North Precinct — Robin Dietz is his name, nice guy, still bothered by it, stays in touch with me — they gave it their best shot, and here we are. So yeah, it was never solved. Why are you asking?"

Kyle waited. Was he really doing this? Did he really think he stood a chance at solving a random street murder the

NYPD had been unable to solve despite putting its best resources to the task under intense local and national pressure?

Yes, yes he did.

"I'd like to look into it."

Skate did not laugh in his face. He did not tell Kyle Callahan he couldn't possibly solve a murder ten detectives, an entire police precinct, and an outraged citizenry could not solve. Instead, he looked up at Kyle and said, "Please do."

That was it: *Please do.* Most polite. Most unfazed.

Skate knew Kyle's story, just as Kyle knew his. He knew Kyle Callahan had stopped the Pride Killer with a bullet to his heart—although for all Skate knew it could have been a bullet to the head or a bullet to the gut. Kyle had had his fleeting notoriety, too. It had made all the papers when Diedrich Kristof Keller III was exposed as the vicious and remarkably successful serial killer who'd terrorized the gay community for seven years (three in absentia). He'd suspected Kyle was a haunted man, just like himself. He couldn't say why. Skate yearned to end the life of the man who'd ended his; but Kyle was Kyle, and Skate felt sorry for him. Some men just don't take well to killing.

"What do you need from me?" Skate said. "To do this, I mean. I know about the Pride Killer."

"Everybody knows," Kyle said.

"I know about the others, too." Skate was referring to the murders at Pride Lodge, and the Pride Gallery killing spree Kyle and some woman had stopped; Skate did not remember her name.

"First we need to talk," Kyle said. "At length, away from here."

Skate thought about it. "I live three blocks from here, at 40th and Eighth."

"The bus depot."

"Across from it, yeah. You free in the morning?"

"Yes," Kyle said. "I don't have to be at work until ten, and it's flexible."

"I get up at noon most days," Skate said. "But I can get up sooner. How about eleven?"

"Eleven it is," said Kyle.

"Meet me on the corner, we'll get coffee and donuts downstairs. Pretty shitty place to have a donut shop, across from the ass of the bus terminal, but it's popular. Lots of donut bags stuffed under bus seats, I guess."

Kyle nodded and took out his wallet. He was anxious to continue the conversation, but not here. They'd been lucky not to have another customer come in—it was still early—and he wanted to move on for the night, to ponder what he'd just gotten himself into, and to figure out how to tell Danny. Then he would tell Detective Linda. Finally he would head to 40th Street and Eighth Avenue and do the one thing he knew would bring him back from the brink of despair: chase a murderer.

"That'll be seven ninety-five," Skate said, ringing up the sale.

"How's Niz?" Kyle asked, taking out a ten dollar bill and handing it to Skate.

"Still trying to marry off his last two daughters. But in a caring way. He's a good man, and they're nice girls. I hope they all find what they're looking for."

Kyle got his change, shoved it into his pocket, said, "See you in the morning," and left.

Skate watched after him. He knew better than to have expectations. He knew this was probably a fool's errand, Kyle Callahan chasing after a street punk who was surely long dead with a syringe in his arm and no one to care. But Skate Copley had no reason not to try, and nothing left to lose.

CHAPTER Three

Kyle Callahan and Danny Durban had been married for almost two years. It wasn't a life Kyle had imagined for himself until it happened. After following his first love David from Chicago to New York thirty-five years ago, then watching it fizzle within months once David realized there were so many men on the menu he had yet to try, Kyle had resigned himself to being single. He stayed that way, too, with a few affairs thrown in every five years or so. Some ended quickly and painlessly, brief experiments that did not have the anticipated results. Others flamed out spectacularly, leaving both men singed. Then, about fifteen years ago, Kyle just gave up. Had he not gone to the photography exhibit of a friend at the Katherine Pride Gallery the same night Danny was there, Kyle would probably still be single and not surprised by it. Life in Brooklyn with his cat had become the life he expected for himself. Then, a chance encounter at the gallery, spilled drinks as Danny came around a corner and bumped into him, a gaze into each other's eyes, and they were married six years later. Or was it seven? Time and the memories it accrued had a way of blurring.

Kyle gave up his apartment in Brooklyn and moved, with a cat and several belongings in tow, into the co-op Danny owned at 25th Street and Lexington Avenue. Kyle never thought Manhattan was all it claimed to be, or that it lived up to its self-generated hype, but it was home. It was where he woke up every day and went to bed every night, and it was where he expected to live happily until the time arrived for them to consider some pleasant retirement community away from the sirens, traffic and hive of people rushing frantically to nowhere. Staring out the small window in their kitchen, he hoped that time would not arrive for another decade or two.

Wednesday was going to be tense. Today was the day the U.S. District Attorney for the Southern District of New York was expected to announce formal charges against Manhattan D.A. Raul Sandoval. That was the huge story Kyle, Imogene and the rest of the New York media were feverishly working on, and an announcement was only the beginning. Sandoval would fight it; standing in solidarity with him would be hundreds of thousands from a city of eight million who had not only voted for him, but placed their dreams and hopes on him. Sandoval was going to change things. Sandoval was a door being kicked open, a ceiling being crashed through. And now, for those who wanted to believe this could not happen, as well as those who'd waited with unconcealed glee for Sandoval's fall, it was about to reach a critical juncture. He would deny the charges, with his long-suffering wife Gloria on one side and his two daughters referred to, if not present. Outrage! Trumped up charges! And, of course, racism. "They" had been out to get him from the day he'd announced his candidacy — so claimed Raul Sandoval and all those who could not admit to themselves he was corrupt. Kyle and Danny were two of those people who had hoped Sandoval would change city politics for the better. He was the D.A, not the mayor or a City Council member, but his presence could have meant a new dawn, had it not brought with it the old shadows of machine politics and backroom favors asked for and exchanged. There was no pleasure for Kyle in seeing Sandoval head slowly to the gallows. He was as weary of corruption in the politicians he voted for as he was of watching their downfalls.

Kyle sat at the kitchen table reading the New York Times. It was the one throwback to a slower time he would not give up until he was forced to, a time of stories "above the fold," newsprint and ink stains on fingers. He had a smartphone; everyone did. He had a Mac on his desk in the spare room, a laptop, an iPad, a Kindle, and, since Christmas, a watch Danny gave him that synced with his phone and did lots of things Kyle hadn't taken the time to figure out. But, damn it, he was going to read his newspaper!

He was on his second cup of coffee when Danny came out of the bedroom trailed by their cats, Smelly and Leonard. Smelly was Kyle's from his life as a bachelor, but she'd turned coat and switched allegiance over the course of his time with Danny. She still loved Kyle, but she loved being able to manipulate Danny more. He gave her treats. He welcomed her into their crowded bed — two men and two cats on a queen mattress was overly cozy for Kyle. Leonard, her housemate and perpetual acquaintance — the cats would never be friends — had been Danny's since being picked from a lineup as a kitten. It was Leonard's apartment, but Smelly never got the memo. She humored Leonard, and at least they didn't fight.

"Morning," Danny said, stepping into the kitchen and reaching for a single-serving K-cup. Kyle had introduced the coffee machine into the household several years ago and still liked trying different flavors, mostly from South American countries.

"Morning," Kyle said.

"Today's the big day."

Kyle looked up. For a moment he thought Danny was talking about the news Kyle was about to give him, then realized that was impossible.

"Oh, you mean about Sandoval," he said.

"Well, yes, I don't know what other big news there is. You didn't get home until after midnight."

Kyle had worked later than he'd wanted to with Imogene on the story. Everything had to be in place, with contingencies: plans A, B, and C. The indictment was not a sure thing until the federal prosecutor said it was. And what if Sandoval jumped out a window? What if his wife, breaking protocol and longstanding tradition, refused to stand by her criminal and left him?

"She's making us wait until this afternoon," Kyle said, referring to Eleanor Duvall, "El from Hell" as her enemies and those she'd targeted called her. The U.S. District Attorney had set her sights on Raul Sandoval two years ago and was known to be meticulous in her indictments.

"Is that unusual, waiting until late in the day?" Danny asked. He finished putting cream in his coffee. As he was about to join Kyle at the small kitchen table, he grabbed a packet of cat snacks from the cabinet and brought them with him. Smelly knew this was coming and was already perched by his chair.

Kyle sighed. They'd resigned themselves to Smelly being a fat cat and did their best just to keep her from becoming obese.

"I don't really know if it's unusual," Kyle said. "Mostly it's just inconvenient. We won't know until the announcement which story to run with, who to call for comment. Imogene has me doing that more now — dialing for scoops, distraught family members, that sort of thing."

Kyle was an excellent personal assistant and liked doing personal-assistant things like travel arrangements and calendar keeping. He'd never wanted to get into the reporting end of things, but since losing his passion for photography he'd welcomed his options and had been glad Imogene offered them. He didn't much care for seeking quotes from people who hated the media, much less the ones looking for justice for a slain loved one in a world where justice was a sound bite, but he was getting more comfortable with it.

"Anything interesting in the paper?" Danny asked. He wasn't big on newspapers, but he always asked Kyle to give him the fine points — it saved him the trouble of having to read it for himself.

"Not really," said Kyle, in a tone suggesting there had been something interesting and he just wasn't saying.

Danny looked at him. After this much time together, these many days and nights in the intimacy of relationship, he knew when Kyle had something more to reveal.

"What is it?" Danny asked.

"What's what?"

"What's the rest of that 'not really?' Is there something you want to tell me? Please don't make it another serial killer, I'm really not up for that."

Danny immediately realized his mistake. He was well aware of the guilt Kyle had felt since shooting Diedrich Keller — the therapy, the nightmares, the brief attempts with anti-depressants.

"I didn't mean — "

"Don't worry about it," Kyle said. He slid the paper to the side. "But yes, there is more."

Kyle cleared his throat; Danny waited.

"I think I want to look into something."

Danny sipped his coffee, keeping his eyes on Kyle over the cup's rim. "Yes?" he said.

"It's not a killer, not some sociopath running around strangling people."

"But?"

"There is no 'but,'" Kyle said. "Okay, I'll just come out with it. There's this guy who works at the deli near my office. His name is Skate Copley — Stuart, I think, but everybody calls him Skate."

The name Copley rang a bell with Danny. He couldn't place it at the moment, but he remembered something in the news about it, someone with that name.

"Anyway," Kyle continued. "His daughter was murdered three years ago and it was never solved."

Now Danny remembered. Corinne Copley had made national news. She'd been the poster child for tough-on-crime types across the country, and especially in New York City. She'd been killed for her phone, nothing more. For several weeks reporters informed the public how dangerous it was to use their iPhones or Androids or whatever else was of any value whatsoever where people could see them and snatch them. Don't wear ear buds, they said—you can't hear the thief coming up on you. Don't carry your phone where it can be easily grabbed. And in Corinne Copley's case, if they want what you have, give it to them.

"What are you telling me?" Danny said.

"I just want to look into it."

"A cold case?"

"Yes," said Kyle. "That's why it's not something for you to worry about. It probably won't go anywhere. The police couldn't solve it, the media couldn't solve it, nobody called in any valuable tips despite, what, $50,000 offered as a reward for information?"

"I see you've been doing some research," Danny said. "What time did Imogene go home?"

Damn him, Kyle thought. He knows me so well. It was true, too: Imogene had headed home just after 11:00 p.m. and Kyle had stayed behind. He'd said he had more work to do on the Sandoval story, but really he'd spent the time online looking back over the Corinne Copley murder.

"Busted," Kyle said. "I stayed later than Imogene just to refresh my memory about this case."

"And what makes you think you can solve it when the NYPD's finest could not?"

"Nothing makes me think that. I just … I need something to bring me back, Danny."

Danny knew exactly what Kyle was talking about. He'd watched his husband sink ever deeper into depression, with a side order of regret at having killed a man in self-defense. His instinct was to tell Kyle to stay as far away from this as possible, but his heart and his head told him differently. If this is what Kyle needed to feel alive again, then so be it. It was a cold case. The killer was a street thug who was most likely dead or moved on to some other city. The odds of Kyle solving this were slim; and even if he did, what would be the harm? He'd tell the police what he knew, what he'd found out, and some cheap crook would spend his life in prison, if he wasn't there already.

"Okay," Danny said. "If this is what you want to do."

Kyle sat up, surprised and relieved at how quickly Danny had come to see his perspective. It couldn't hurt anything to look into the girl's death. It would give him something to put his mind to. And it was ... dare he say it? ... exciting.

"But," said Danny, holding up a finger, "I want you to talk to Detective Linda about this."

Linda Sikorsky was retired from the New Hope, Pennsylvania, police force, but Kyle still insisted on calling her Detective Linda. They'd met when she was investigating the murders at Pride Lodge. She and Kyle became fast friends and she'd been his accomplice — for what else could they call it? — during the Katherine Pride Gallery murders, the awful mess at CrossCreek Farm near her home in New Jersey, and in that basement with the Pride Killer. On the one hand, Danny thought the two of them attracted trouble, on the other hand he wanted her involved in anything dangerous Kyle might get himself into. A three year old murder was still a murder.

"Agreed," said Kyle. "As a matter of fact, I'm Skyping with her this morning."

Danny felt like he'd just been played. Kyle had planned to do as Kyle wanted to do all along. He sighed.

"Then what?"

"Then I'm meeting with Skate Copley at his apartment later this morning to go over everything and see if there's anything there to follow, any direction to take. After that I'll go to work and be busy with the Raul Sandoval story for the rest of the day."

Danny nodded. There was nothing more to say for now. He secretly hoped Kyle could not solve this one, that a case this cold would stay frozen and buried. And if not, he hoped there was no one waiting at the end of it to tell Kyle he should have minded his own business.

"Let's go, kids," Danny said to the cats.

He took his coffee and the packet of treats and headed back into the bedroom, trailed by the two traitorous animals who only seemed interested in Kyle when he had something to feed them.

CHAPTER Four

An hour later Kyle was seated at his computer, showered and dressed for the day. Danny was milling about in the apartment, moving from bedroom to living room to kitchen, doing one thing or another as was his habit until he left for work at Margaret's Passion sometime around 11:00 a.m. Margaret's was the restaurant he and Kyle owned, having bought it from Margaret Bowman a year and a half earlier. Margaret had since moved to Florida to spend her remaining years with her sister, and Danny pretty much ran the restaurant on his own with the help of a topnotch and dedicated staff—Kyle was no restaurateur and had no desire to be one. It was Danny's baby, the place where Danny had worked for twelve years, where he'd served and loved the old woman faithfully, and where he lived his passion. His *Margaret's Passion*. It made him happy; that's all Kyle cared about.

The door was closed. This was their second bedroom that they'd made into a shared office, although it belonged mostly to Kyle. His late father's desk took up nearly half of one wall, nestled beneath a window overlooking Lexington Avenue five stories below. There was a smaller desk Danny sometimes used, and several file cabinets they shared. There was also a sofa bed against the wall just to the right of the door. This was where their occasional guests slept, including Kyle's mother Sally when she visited from Chicago, and Detective Linda when she was in town. Kyle was just about to call her on Skype; that's why the door was closed. Normally when he called her he would leave the door open so Danny could pop in and say hello, but today he wanted to fill her in on his decision about the cold case and get her advice—although he might not take it. If she told him to leave it alone he would humor her and pursue it anyway. But he didn't think that would happen. He and Linda had become partners in crime solving and he suspected she'd be as interested in the story as he was once he gave her the details.

It was an interesting relationship. Linda was the only lesbian Kyle had as a close friend. He knew plenty of them, but he hadn't been this close with any since high school. It made him think of Tina, the large girl he was tight with his senior year. Her nickname was Fat Tina, something she knew and Kyle believed she'd hated while pretending to laugh it off. Tina knew he liked boys. He knew she liked food and petite cheerleaders. They both liked speed, and Tina was a great source of diet pills she got from her doctor. They didn't curb her appetite, but they provided her and Kyle with many especially energetic afternoons. He was wondering whatever became of Tina when he glanced at the clock on his Mac and realized he was five minutes late calling Linda.

He pulled up the Skype application, found Linda's avatar and clicked "video call."

Three ring attempts and up popped Detective Linda.

"You're late," she said.

She was smiling. Kyle had that effect on her. Just as Linda was the only lesbian Kyle could say was really part of his life, Kyle was one of only two gay men—Danny being the other—she could say were an intimate part of hers. (While she thought the world of her assistant store manager Mitchell Parsons, she had not known him long enough to consider him an intimate friend, nor did she think it was wise to get too familiar with someone who worked for you.)

Linda and her wife Kirsten McClellan came as a pair, but as with most people whose close friends had partners, the partner was part of the package. Kyle liked Kirsten; he might even say he loved her at this point. But the core of the relationship would always be Kyle and Linda. Were either of them ever to be alone again (neither believed divorce would be the cause), Kyle knew their friendship would go on.

"You look good in your pajamas," Kyle said. "Are those new?"

It was Linda's usual attire when they Skyped this early in the morning. Linda owned a "vintage everything" store in New Hope, Pennsylvania, about twenty minutes from her house in the woods on the Jersey side of the Delaware River. She'd retired after twenty years on the New Hope police force and opened the store, named *For Pete's Sake* after her late cop father. Kyle was as delighted as she was the business had survived into its second year.

"Kirsten got them for me in Philly," Linda said. "We spent a long weekend with my mother. She's fine, before you ask."

Kyle was glad to hear it. He knew Linda and her mother were close. Kirsten's mother had died from metastasized breast cancer the year before. It had been hard on both women and Kyle automatically wondered if Linda's mother was all right.

Linda sipped coffee from a mug, then said to Kyle, "It's Wednesday. So what did you want to talk about?"

Their calls were always on Friday, when they could catch up from the week. Kyle had texted her from work the night before. He'd planned to do this whether or not Danny approved of his newest mission, and was greatly relieved things had gone his way.

"I've been seeing a therapist for six months," Kyle said.

Linda knew this. She'd had many conversations with Kyle about his feelings over the shooting. She'd been a cop for twenty years, a homicide detective for the last six of them, and she was no stranger to death. Just as importantly, she'd been a very tough woman her entire adult life and did not harbor the misgivings, regret or guilt Kyle was feeling. She was comfortable with guns. She voted Republican, unless a candidate was awful or corrupt, which was often the case, and she paid little mind to dead serial killers. She was only surprised at how many she'd come to know since meeting Kyle.

"I know you've been seeing a therapist," she said. "Did you have some kind of breakthrough? Did you realize Diedrich Keller's death isn't worth torturing yourself over?"

"Yes and no," replied Kyle. "But that's not why we're talking. What I realized was that I needed something to get me going again. Something to reinvigorate me."

Linda peered at him a moment through the webcam. "You're taking up photography again?" she said hopefully.

She's a perceptive one, Kyle thought. She knows this isn't about photography or taking up painting or travel writing.

"It's a case," he said.

"A case? A case of *what*?"

"A cold case."

"Ahh, Kyle," she said. "Are you sure about this?"

"I'm very sure, Detective."

Linda rolled her eyes. She'd accepted that Kyle would always call her Detective Linda, probably into their eighties, but she did not consider herself a detective anymore. She was a store owner, a wife, and a country girl living in the woods.

"So what's this case about?" Linda finally asked.

"That's why I called you," he said.

"I know that. We've got that out of the way. Now tell me the particulars. And specifically, tell me there's no psychopath waiting with a switchblade at the end of this road."

Kyle told her then—about Skate Copley, his daughter, her murder, and the crime that had sent chills throughout New York City and beyond. An unsolved homicide, a dead teenager killed for a piece of plastic and circuitry.

As Kyle gave Linda the details he could see her interest sparking. The call had done what he'd hoped, even though he'd not expressed this hope to anyone. Linda was seventy miles away in a small house surrounded by trees. But she was only a moment away in digital time, a face and voice he could talk to any time of the day or night with just a click of his mouse and a webcam. He'd wanted to hook her into this, and he had.

He would need all the help he could get.

CHAPTER Five

Manhattan's Port Authority Bus Terminal was built in 1950 to consolidate the many bus stations then dotting the city. Occupying the blocks between 40th and 42nd Streets south to north, and Eighth and Ninth Avenues east to west, it was as ugly a landmark as one could find in any major city. It not only lacked Grand Central's grandeur or Penn Station's subterranean blandness, it was also not a place anyone wanted to be. You *might* want to go to Penn Station; after all, Madison Square Garden was there. And Grand Central was a world-renowned gem, restored into one of the city's prime destinations for local residents as well as tourists. But Port Authority? It was a place where buses fumed billowing trails of stink behind them, and where tired commuters and budget travelers went to find a seat on long, uncomfortable, rolling tubes. No one would go to the bus terminal who didn't have to be there for one reason or another, and often the reason was one they'd happily trade for never having to ride a bus again.

Kyle could see the terminal's backside as he walked north on Ninth Avenue. Skate had emailed him his address that morning, and after having a light breakfast at home, watching the news on TV, and over-thinking what he was about to get into, he headed out at 10:15 to walk there. Forty-five minutes gave him more than enough time to make the trip. It also gave him time to analyze the situation and realize he was taking this on from scratch with a high probability of failure. There was no serial killer to catch at the end of a nightmarish rainbow; no devious murderer to match wits against. As far as anyone had known for three years since Corinne Copley's murder, there was just a junkie somewhere, dead or alive, who'd had a gun when a seventeen-year-old girl was on the wrong street at the wrong time. And he, Kyle Callahan, thought he could do what the best detectives in the city could not. Well, actually, he didn't think that. He only thought he would try, and to start this impossible mission he needed to learn everything he could from Skate Copley.

While there are no affordable neighborhoods left in Manhattan, there are still some that look like they should be. The Lower East Side, Washington Heights, and certainly Hell's Kitchen. Just because the rents there were now commensurate with the rest of a city in love with wealth, it didn't mean the place looked any nicer. The buildings that had been abandoned, the warehouses and storefronts, all looked the same as they had thirty, forty, or fifty years ago. The money that had gone into turning some of them into high-end condos and most of them into insanely expensive apartments had not been spent on their exteriors. The place *looked* cheap. It looked dirty. It looked like street gangs might still rule the sidewalks and avenues, but there'd been no gangs for a very long time. All of Manhattan had been converted into a tourist-friendly vacation destination most tourists only came to gawk at and leave. A nice place to say you'd visited, but not a place for decent folk to linger.

Kyle found himself standing on the corner of 40th Street and Ninth Avenue, directly across from the bus terminal's back entrance. An overpass built for buses provided shelter to homeless men and women, a respite for those with no jobs to go to during the day and nothing better to do at night than mill around with their friends in a sort of open air arcade for the destitute. Kyle worked not far from here, about three blocks, but he seldom had reason to venture north to where he was now. Manhattan was like that: you could be on a block lined with historic brownstones one minute, and ten minutes later find yourself among a row of old empty factories.

This particular corner was an emptying-out station just east of the Lincoln Tunnel. Cars entered the city in a steady flow; more noticeably, buses crawled one after another along 40th Street, belching their exhaust up into the air and snarling traffic at the best of times.

Kyle looked up and saw Skate in a fourth floor window, his head stuck out and his arm waving.

"I thought you were going to meet me on the corner," Kyle called up.

"I got donuts and coffee already, couldn't sleep," Skate yelled back. "I'll come down."

Kyle was surprised the building had an intercom. It looked like a property the landlord had neglected for years. The windows were all filthy, and had Skate not had his open, Kyle would never have seen him through the grimy glass. He walked to the building's front door and waited. After a moment he could hear Skate bounding down the steps. It wasn't something he'd connected with Skate before — bounding. Skate was a depressive, or at least that's how most people experienced him these days. The skinny, quiet older guy making sandwiches and toasted bagels behind the 38-Nine Deli counter, sometimes with Niz Ramani working the cash register or stocking shelves, but most times alone. Kyle wondered if taking on this case had given Skate hope; was that why he was jumping the steps three at a time, hurrying down to meet Kyle? And was it a mistake, a terrible thing to offer a man when hope was probably slim or nonexistent?

Skate got to the inner door and waved again. Like many apartment buildings it had two doors: the exterior door, and then, a few feet in, a second door. Skate yanked them open one after the other and let Kyle into the building.

It was as bleak inside as it was outside. A row of rusted mailboxes lined one wall, with a first floor apartment in the back behind the stairs. There was no elevator — it was a walkup. So they did, walking slowly up (they did not bound back up the stairs), with Skate in the lead.

"Did you have breakfast?" Skate said over his shoulder as he led the way.

"I did, thank you," Kyle replied. He didn't say he was hesitant to eat in this building, concerned the grime of the place might seep into his food.

"Coffee? I've got some crullers from the donut shop. A little greasy but delicious."

"I'll take you up on the coffee," Kyle said. He didn't know how long he'd be there; he should accept something Skate offered him.

They got to the fourth floor landing and Kyle noticed he was winded. He made a mental note to himself, stacking it with a thousand others saying exactly the same thing: get in shape. He was well into his fifties and determined not to be creaking, huffing, and reaching for the grab bar at sixty.

There were four apartments on each floor. Skate reached the top of the stairs, circled back around them and opened the door to 4C.

Following Skate into the apartment, Kyle noticed immediately how sparse, clean and orderly it was. The walls were completely bare. The window from which Skate had waved down to Kyle had sheer drapes. There was no air conditioner, and Kyle wondered how Skate lived through Manhattan summers without one. Maybe he had a fan stored in the closet—he must; the heat and humidity were too much for any sentient being to survive without at least a breeze.

There was a tiny kitchen, a tiny stove, a tiny refrigerator, and when Skate went to get the coffee and donuts from the tiny countertop, he was the only one who could fit in the space.

"Please," said Skate from the kitchen, "make yourself comfortable.

Easier said than done, thought Kyle, not unkindly. He walked into the living room, realizing immediately it was also the bedroom. This was a studio apartment; the bed was a foldout doubling as an old plaid couch on which Kyle quickly took a seat. There was a matching armchair opposite the couch, and a coffee table between them. An ancient analog television sat atop a crate on the floor. It appeared not to have cable.

Skate came back in, set their cups on the coffee table, and perched on the edge of the armchair cushion, his arms resting on his knees as he leaned forward.

"I didn't ask if you wanted milk or sugar," Skate said. "Do you?"

"Black's fine."

Skate reached for his cup, took a sip and put it back on a coaster.

"So ..." Skate said. "You think you can actually find the guy who killed my baby?"

It was blunt and wasted no time getting to the point of why Kyle was here.

"I want to try," said Kyle. He sipped his own coffee to be polite, careful not to grimace at the taste. He'd not had black coffee for a very long time.

"What do you need from me?" Skate said.

"I need to know whatever you know. Everything you know. Every single detail you can give me."

Skate nodded, biting his lower lip. "I have a file," he said.

The Details:

Corinne Copley was seventeen years old when her life ended abruptly on 37th Street, between Eighth and Ninth Avenues. April 23rd, Tuesday, three years ago. She'd been walking west, headed for Maria's Cantina to meet her friend Gilda Fleischman to celebrate Gilda's eighteenth birthday with a small circle of friends. These friends did not include Lydia Becker, with whom Corinne had spent the day. The two girls had skipped school to have lunch at Manhattan's most celebrated, newest, must-go restaurant at the time. The fact of skipping school complicated things and was not known until after Corinne's death. Such are the twists of fate that can lead to a gunshot on a sparsely populated side street in Hell's Kitchen. Another twist of fate: Lydia was not invited to the dinner party. That's why Corinne was alone. Lydia did not know there was a dinner party, and Corinne didn't tell her.

After the girls had lunch at Constantine, *the* restaurant, located in the newly opened and widely publicized Oasis hotel (covered in every magazine that mattered to those who mattered), the girls split up. Lydia went home, frustrated that they'd not been able to post any of their pictures to social media (remember, they were skipping school, and both girls' parents had the extremely annoying habit of following them on every social network the girls joined), and thoroughly disappointed with Constantine. No celebrity worth taking a selfie with had been there; the restaurant's hotness had cooled in six months of operation, and both girls felt let down.

Rather than go home herself, Corinne decided to see a movie in Chelsea to pass the afternoon. When that was over it would be time to head to Maria's Cantina. Which she did, dying along the way.

At one point as she headed to dinner, about halfway up the block on 37th Street, she took a call from her father. He was a doter, a fretter. He stayed in touch with his daughter frequently, and had been frustrated by her lack of communication that day. He did not know she'd skipped school. It wasn't like Corinne Copley to take the outlaw way.

"I'm fine, Daddy," she'd said. "School was school, it's pretty much the same from day to day."

"Where are you now?" Skate asked. He was at his office at Barton and Loman, staring out from seventeen floors above the city, squeezing a rubber ball in his left hand. His job as one of their top financial managers placed a lot of stress in his life, and he tried to channel it down his arm, through his hand and into the ball a dozen times a day.

"I'm on Thirty-Seventh," she said.

He was not pleased. "I told you to stay off the side streets when you're out there. Take Thirty-Fourth, lots of pedestrians. You're in Hell's Kitchen, Baby, it's not the best place."

He could not see Corinne roll her eyes.

"Everywhere's safe in New York City now," she said. And then she heard footsteps hurrying up behind her.

Skate drained his coffee like a man with an addiction to it. He looked as if he was going to offer Kyle another cup, then realized Kyle had barely touched his.

"What happened next?" Kyle asked.

"I heard her talking to someone," Skate said. "For just a second. And I said, 'Corinne, who are you talking to?' I could tell she was angry. She came back on and said, 'Daddy, he wants my phone.' 'Who wants your phone?' I said. I heard a man's voice, but I couldn't make out the words. Then Corinne said, 'Fuck you,' something I'd never heard her say."

Skate went silent, his eyes shifting to the floor.

"Then what?" Kyle asked quietly.

"She yelled, 'Let go,' and then the gunshot." Skate slowly looked back up. "I kept saying, 'Speak to me, Baby, speak to me.'"

Skate Copley had been talking to his daughter when she was shot in the head. She never spoke to him again, never responded to his final plea.

"It's what wakes me up in the middle of the night," Skate said. "Every night, for three years. 'Speak to me,' over and over. But she never does and she never will."

Kyle hoped that three years had given Skate enough time to talk about it rationally — or at least objectively.

"You think she was killed for her phone?" Kyle said.

"Oh, yes. They knew that right away. It didn't have a kill switch. You know what that is?"

Kyle knew. It was a built-in mechanism on a smartphone that allowed the owner to essentially destroy the phone remotely, making it useless to a thief. Legislation had been proposed — and opposed by manufacturers — more than once. It seemed stolen phones were a money maker for phone manufacturers, too. A stolen phone means the purchase of a new one. But people had lost their lives, including Corinne

Copley. Her death had brought the matter to the national forefront once again, and finally the major phone manufacturers were making new devices with kill switches. Even they couldn't ignore the cold blooded killing of a teenager for her phone.

"I think I'd like to stop now," Kyle said.

Skate had given him a large manila envelope stuffed with newspaper reports, online printouts and handwritten notes.

"Now?" Skate said, surprised. "But ..."

Kyle held up his hand. "We'll talk again," he said. "I just want to absorb all this. Get my own thoughts about it going. Read through what you've given me."

"It's everything I could find," Skate said. "Everything I could get my hands on, including police reports, witness accounts."

Kyle was startled. Civilians did not usually have copies of police reports.

"I have a friend in the Department," Skate said. "Detective Robin Dietz. He felt sorry for me."

"Well, let me have a look at it all and see what I can find, if anything."

Skate nodded. It made sense. If he kept talking, he would start filling Kyle's head with his own suspicions, ideas and frustrations.

"Where are you going to start?" he said.

Kyle held up the envelope. "With this."

It wasn't yet noon and Kyle had felt his phone vibrating every ten minutes for an hour. Imogene was trying to reach him. Maybe Raul Sandoval had been indicted. Or maybe he'd taken a dive off the 59th Street Bridge. That was unlikely, given Sandoval's ego and chutzpah. Or maybe Imogene was just being Imogene and pestering Kyle with her needs. She was a needy boss and an equally needy friend. It was one of the things he liked about her—that she seemed to require him to maintain her own equilibrium in life.

"I'm sorry but I have to go," Kyle said.

"I understand, you have to get to work. Me, too, in about eight hours."

"I'll see you if I'm working late again." Kyle stood up from the couch, the envelope in his hand. "But I kind of hope not. I don't enjoy working nights, and Danny doesn't care much for it, either."

Skate had never met Kyle's husband Danny. "Does he know about this?"

"I told him this morning."

"And he's okay with it?"

"Don't worry about it, Skate. Don't worry about anything. Just give me some time to read through everything and I'll stop by the deli again. No later than Friday, I promise."

"That's the day, you know."

"The day?" Then it hit Kyle: Friday was April 23rd, three years since Corinne Copley had spoken to her father for the last time. "I didn't realize . . ."

"It's all right. Why would the anniversary mean anything to anyone but me? The rest of the world moved on, I understand that."

Skate hurried to the dresser by the window, the room's only other piece of furniture besides a small book case. He took a pad of yellow paper, a pen from a coffee can, and wrote down his cell phone number.

"Here," he said, handing the paper to Kyle. "I'm available, twenty-four-seven. Seriously. I don't sleep much."

Kyle took the paper and looked at him. No, he thought, I imagine you don't sleep much, and he wondered again if he was doing the right thing. Once he started down this road there was no turning back, not until he found the truth at the end of it—even if the truth was that there was nothing to be found.

"I'll talk to you soon," Kyle said. He slipped the paper with Skate's phone number into his pants pocket and headed for the door.

Skate saw him out, waving a last time as Kyle headed for the stairs. He closed the door, listening to Kyle's footsteps descending flight after flight out of the building.

A moment later he sat on his plaid couch in his small apartment, located two blocks from where everything that mattered to him had died, and he cried.

CHAPTER Six

Kyle was alone at work later that morning. Imogene and her cameraman Stanley were already downtown. U.S. District Attorney Eleanor Duvall had announced a three-page indictment against Raul Sandoval mid-morning—something Kyle missed while he spoke with Skate Copley about his daughter's murder—and Sandoval, true to form, was turning it into an outdoor circus on the Courthouse steps. Kyle could see it playing on the TV monitors in the small newsroom. He turned down the sound on the set closest to him, just around the other side of the cubicle wall on Imogene's desk, and thanked good timing for having the office to himself. He was probably in trouble with Imogene for being late without notice; he'd deal with that later. He had no intention of telling her what he was doing. She was a newshound. In fact, the rise in her career had paralleled Kyle's involvement with crime: the murders he solved were the ones Imogene covered to such great success. Kyle had reluctantly given her an exclusive interview after the death of the Pride Killer. She did not know he'd since spent six months in therapy telling Peter Benoit what it was *really* like to end a man's life, and working out the emotional and psychological price he'd paid for it.

He'd stopped at the 38-Nine Deli for coffee and a toasted bagel. The owner Niz was behind the cash register with his nephew Josef on sandwich duty. Kyle didn't know Niz well enough to engage in more than passing conversation with him, so he just commented on the spring weather. It was finally warm again in New York City after a brutally cold winter that had climate deniers crowing about the Polar Vortex—a circling mass of ice masquerading as air—while polar bears drowned in melting glaciers.

"That's really something," Niz had said, glancing up at the small television set mounted on the wall behind the front counter.

Kyle had glanced up and seen Raul Sandoval preening for the cameras, an odd gesture for a man facing prison time for bribery.

Kyle had nodded, yes, that was really something, then thanked Niz and taken his bagel and coffee back onto the street for the two block walk to work.

The envelope Skate gave him was old and dirty. Skate's hands had opened it hundreds of times, removing and replacing the things Kyle was now taking out and spreading on his desk. Half of the two-dozen items were newspaper clippings: the New York Times, the Post, USA Today, and an article in Time Magazine about the dangers of displaying smartphones, tablets and iPods in public. Somebody might grab it; somebody might shoot you in the head. One young woman had been shoved onto the subway tracks, the thief escaping with her phone while she screamed at an oncoming train. The scream did nothing to stop it and the woman died in two pieces, one on each side of the tracks.

Also in the envelope was a photocopied police report and, to Kyle's shock, an autopsy report. These were not things a family member would have. An attorney, perhaps, but not the father of a murder victim. Kyle immediately thought of the detective Skate told him about—what was his name? Robin Dietz? Kyle grabbed a pen and a pad of paper and wrote the man's name down, guessing on the spelling until he could find it in the reports. He wondered if Dietz had secretly passed on information to Skate in his frustration at not solving the case. He would have been expected to move on; there were other murders to solve, other beasts to hunt. Kyle would have to speak to the detective at some point.

There were also a dozen pages from a yellow legal pad, covered in scribbling and notes from Skate. There were angry doodles, etched into the paper as Skate (so Kyle imagined) drew circles and spirals trying to think his way around a problem with no solution. At the top of the first page Skate had written "Speak to me" in block letters. Those words again, that unanswered plea.

The second page contained several names. People involved? People to question? People in whom the police, and Skate, had placed their hopes only to have them crushed as the investigation went nowhere?

Lydia Becker. Gilda Fleischman. Constantine. And then notations, "Talk to ticket taker at Chelsea movies," and "Find counterman at bakery."

The next note startled him: "Stomach contents." Two words with no context. He had a feeling he would find out what the notation meant when he read the autopsy report.

The last three pages were a journal of some sort. Kyle recognized its nature immediately. He wondered if he should continue reading, and why Skate would include something so personal in the envelope. Maybe he forgot they were there. Or maybe he wanted Kyle—or anyone who read them—to know the depth of his anguish:

My friends ask me why I stay in this city, those few friends I have left. I tell them there's no escaping the sound of her voice. It doesn't matter where I am or where I might go. It's an echo that always comes back to me, and like an echo from across a canyon, I can't see where it came from anymore. I can't see her. I know she's there, calling out for me, calling out for help, wondering why I'm not there to stop what happened. But I'm not, and I wasn't, and there's no denying that. No train could take me far enough, no plane high enough—even into orbit, if I could go there. Even into the far reaches of space. Her voice would find me, calling, 'Daddy, Daddy … where are you?' and I'd have to answer, 'Here,' but not there. I wasn't there that night. I can never be there. So I stay.

And the friends I don't have anymore, which is most of them, would tell me to move on, that a man can't live on vengeance and grief alone. They're right about the grief part. It kills you; it doesn't sustain you. It wears you down and smothers you with guilt because you believe you could have prevented it. Grief because it happened, guilt because you're convinced it was somehow your fault. But vengeance? I have to disagree. A man can live on it. It can keep a man going, the way it's kept me going for three years. Wanting it. Needing it. Knowing even if it never comes it kept me alive. It's been my reason for living, and unlike the friends I no longer have, it never goes away.

Corinne was only seventeen when she spoke to me the last time. Hers is the voice that echoes through these years. She'd been so happy, out for a night on the town with friends she was meeting for dinner. The restaurant she was going to isn't there anymore. Maria's Cantina. Come and gone like so many things in this come-and-go city. Corinne's gone, too, but she was happy and alive that night. It was April 23rd, still cool. Some days we never forget, like the day a child is born, or the day our belief in everything dies.

Giving her that phone was like giving her the gun that ended her life. Like introducing her to the man who took it. Guilt corrodes the soul, but there's nothing I can do to end it. Well, maybe one thing, but I'm still waiting for that. Waiting to find him. I'm ready. I don't need much but my bare hands.

I fretted on my daughter. Some would say too much, I would say not nearly enough. Had I worried just a little bit more I might have gone with her, made sure she arrived at her destination unharmed. But she didn't like me hovering and hounding. She believed she was an adult now. I knew better, but I didn't correct her.

April 23rd, a perfect evening. I called her at six-thirty. She was walking along 37th Street, headed to the restaurant. I always told her to take busy streets, 34th or 42nd, stay in the crowds and the light if it was night. It wasn't dark yet. She ignored me.

'Where are you, Corinne?' I asked.

'Don't worry, Daddy. I'm a big girl now.'

'I didn't ask you if you were a big girl. I asked you where you are.'

'Thirty-Seventh,' she said.

'That's a side street. I told you to stay off the side streets.'

We talked for just another minute. I knew I couldn't keep her on the line long; kids don't want to talk to their parents any longer than they have to, not when they're out for a night with friends in Manhattan.

I'd just told her that her mother was planning a trip to Boston when I heard her talking to someone on the street.

'Excuse me?' she said, as if a stranger had asked for directions.

'Corinne? Who are you talking to?'

'Hey!' she shouted. 'Hey, that's my phone!' Then, to me, 'Daddy, he wants my phone! It's brand new!'

'Who wants your phone?'

'Fuck you!' she shouted. She was in trouble and I was not there.

'Corinne, give him your phone, just give him your phone.'

'Let go!' she shrieked. And then a pop. A single loud pop.

It's the sound that wakes me up at midnight every night of my life. POP!

A gunshot. Not like on TV. More like a party favor from hell. POP!

'Corinne? Corinne? Speak to me.'

Those were the last words I said to her, 'Speak to me.' Once, twice, then shouting it, 'Speak to me!'

They're the words that startle me from sleep in the dark of night, the words I rise to.

Speak to me.

Words that ache, repeating hundreds of times, thousands, in a short, brutal, endless repetition.

Speak to me …

She never did again. The last words I heard her say were telling a stranger on a dark street to let go of her. Let go.

But I can't and I won't. It has cost me everything. It's remarkable how far a life can descend in such a short time, how unrecognizable it can become. Good riddance. My friends are gone. My wife is gone. My job is gone. And I don't care. What I care about has eluded me all this time, but I believe I can see it in the distance. There, walking along 37th Street, just up ahead. A thief. A thief who stole my daughter and whose soul I will someday take in payment, wrap in my daughter's obituary, and set on fire.

Kyle put the pages aside, shaken by the anger and despair in them. He was also struck by how articulate Skate Copley was. Kyle knew the story, the fall from grace, if you consider achievement and wealth to be grace. But still, he admitted to himself, he knew Skate as the man behind the deli counter, the guy who said little and worked the overnight shift. He realized at that moment why Skate did it. He wanted to be there, in the darkest hours, watching. He wanted to think that someday, at some moment when the city was sleeping, the man who killed his daughter would walk into the 38-Nine Deli and Skate would know him for who and what he was. No words to speak between them. Skate would just *know*. And he would kill the man on the spot with nothing but his fists.

Is that what Kyle wanted? To find the man who did this so Skate could have his revenge? It wouldn't play out that way, Kyle knew. If where he was headed led anywhere, it would end with the police making an arrest and a broken father ... not healing, that was impossible ... but being not quite so broken anymore.

You're heading into a cul-de-sac, Kyle, he told himself. If the police and Skate could not find where this information led, why did he think he could? It was clear Skate had made solving his daughter's murder his life's obsession, at the cost of all else his life had once been. It was also clear the killer of his daughter remained at large, dead or otherwise long gone. But still, Kyle was feeling renewed. And feeling guilty for it. Was he ill? Did he really need to immerse himself in murder and casual depravity to feel alive again?

Yes, yes I do.

He began quietly repeating Skate's last words to his child: Speak to me. Speak to me. Over and over, making those three words a mantra he hoped would show him something, anything, that could lay a path for him to follow.

He picked up the police report and began reading.

CHAPTER Seven

Linda Sikorsky was distracted—troubled might be more accurate. Ever since her video call with Kyle that morning she'd had a bad feeling. She and Kyle were very close friends now; not best friends, she reserved that place of pride for her wife Kirsten. But Kyle was certainly a close second and she was uncomfortable with him pursuing a murderer without her, however cold the case may be.

They'd been involved in stopping four killers over the past three years—more if you counted Bo Sweetzer, the one who got away from Pride Lodge, and Sonny Gaines, who killed on his mother's behalf in the dreadful CrossCreek Farm affair. Even more numerous were the victims, some of whom would be alive had Kyle and Linda moved faster. Granted, this case was unsolved; it was unlikely to bring Kyle face to face with anyone more dangerous than an opportunistic street criminal who would be arrested by the police and convicted after a jury deliberated for twenty minutes. It was still a murder investigation, and while it had gone nowhere, there was the slight chance Kyle might find some thread to follow, some detail that led him down a path the others had missed, and Linda did not want Kyle heading down that path alone.

"Boss, you look lost," Mitchell said.

Mitchell Parsons had been the assistant store manager at *For Pete's Sake* since two weeks after its opening. Starting her own business had been a dream of Linda's for many years, to be pursued once she left the New Hope Police Force. She hadn't known what that business would be, only that she would name it after her father. Then, several years ago, she was shopping in Doylestown and came across a store run by a woman named Suzanne. It had everything: vintage clothes, old knick-knacks, even political buttons from a dozen conventions spanning fifty years. A *vintage-everything* store. It quickly became a favorite Saturday destination for her and she'd go there once a month to buy, browse, and befriend the store's owner.

"You could do this, you know," Suzanne told her one afternoon.

Linda knew her time on the force was running out and she'd talked to Suzanne several times about what her next move would be, or, as Suzanne called it, her "next adventure." Linda loved the small store packed floor-to-ceiling with odds and ends, the display case in front with buttons, barrettes, tie clips, all of them in good shape and radiating memories.

"You really think so?" Linda had said to her. "But what if I fail?"

"You won't know if you don't try," Suzanne replied. "And more importantly, there is no failure in trying."

There is no failure in trying.

The simple advice stuck with her. It helped her risk a first relationship at the age of forty-two, meeting then-real estate broker Kirsten McClellan at a New Year's Eve party. The women were now married and living in a small house in the New Jersey woods Linda inherited from her aunt. She had tried a relationship and not failed. She'd moved from New Hope to rural New Jersey, trading life in an apartment for life among trees and deer, and not failed. And she had opened *For Pete's Sake*, unsure how to even begin running a business, and she had not failed.

Linda turned to Mitchell, who was carefully inserting a small shipment of bowties into one of the two tall glass cases to the left of the front door, and said, "I'm not lost, Mitch. I just think I need to go to the City."

Everyone within a hundred miles of New York City called it "the City." Capital-C. When someone said the City, they did not mean Philadelphia, even though it was closer. They certainly didn't mean New Hope or Lambertville or Trenton. There was only one Capital-C-City and Linda had decided to make a trip there.

"Would you be okay if I visited Kyle and Danny for a few days?" Linda asked.

Mitchell knew Kyle and Danny very well. They'd been to visit a half dozen times and even included Mitchell in a few lunches with Linda and Kirsten. (Linda had no problem putting up the "Closed" sign; life was too short to worry about a lost customer or two.) They'd told him how they'd met, literally bumping into each other at the Katherine Pride Gallery. They'd tried to encourage him to date, assuring him it was never too late, something of which he, as a single gay man in his forties, wasn't convinced. It was okay with him; he had his dog Millie and his aquarium, and he knew (so he told himself) that love finds you, you do not find it. He also knew that Linda visiting Kyle could lead to headlines, violence and dead bodies.

"Aren't I always okay when you go away?" Mitchell said. "Are you taking Kirsten with you?"

Linda frowned. Her next conversation would have to be with her wife, who was at home right now working on a novel. Kirsten McClellan had sold her half of McClellan and Powers Real Estate to Madeline Powers. They'd started the business together, but when Kirsten found herself married and living in the woods with a retired homicide detective, she, too, thought it was time for a big change, a next adventure. So she sold the business to Madeline, had her name removed from the door and awning, and spent several months trying to decide what she wanted to do with her life. She tried painting. She tried working at *For Pete's Sake*. She even tried shooting — guns, that is — at the gun club just down the road from Linda's house. None of it stuck; none of it got inside her the way selling property had, with the rush of success and the odd sense of power that came with closing a sale. And then she'd found a website for writers that welcomed novices, or, as Kirsten called it then, wannabes. She wrote a few short stories and got the bug. She joined a local writers group that met every Tuesday night to read and critique each other's work while they drank wine and coffee. And now, in a giant leap of faith and hope in her own abilities, she was writing a novel. A novel about a lesbian detective who lived in Philadelphia, a detective named Roxanne Harmony. Everybody called her Rox ("Roxy" would get you a lecture and possibly handcuffs from the fictional badass). She was Linda in thin disguise. Linda did her best to remain neutral about it; she wanted Kirsten to have a passion, regardless of any outward measure of success. The only thing she'd said for the past six months while Kirsten wrote a first draft of a first Roxanne Harmony mystery was, "Don't ever call me Rox."

Linda sighed and slipped off the stool behind the cash register. "It's a solo trip this time," she said. "I'll tell Kirsten when I get home in about twenty minutes."

Mitchell glanced at the wall calendar. It was Wednesday.

"So should I expect you back by Saturday?" Weekends were the busiest at the store, with tourists pouring into New Hope.

"Let's just say yes," Linda said. She hoped it wouldn't take longer than that. She would not tell Kyle this, but she was trusting he would quickly realize the futility of trying to solve a three-year-old cold case. Kyle would tell Skate Copley he'd done his best, and maybe Mr. Copley would finally let go, however slowly or painfully.

Linda went into the small coat closet behind the cash register and took out her windbreaker. It was warm enough now to wear light jackets. She felt for her keys in the pocket. Then she gave Mitchell a hug and told him she'd call when she got to New York in the morning. She could have stayed the rest of the day but she was restless, and she wanted to catch Kirsten early. It might take some time to convince her the trip was safe, there was no Pride Killer waiting in Manhattan as there had been the last time. She even planned on making dinner, something special to soften Kirsten up and weaken her resistance to the trip. She would leave in the morning.

Kirsten would know she was going regardless of any objections and accept it. Kyle would not know Linda was coming until she knocked on his door. He was the one person she didn't want telling her not to make the trip, to stay away this time, it's just an old, cold murder.

She'd had the sense from the first details Kyle gave her that morning that no murder is ever truly cold. It only cools to an ember, and from a single ember a fire can roar to life.

CHAPTER Eight

The sidewalk on 37th Street appeared no different from any other in Manhattan, yet this was where Corinne Copley lost her life and where Kyle now stood, looking first toward Eighth Avenue, then turning and peering west toward Ninth. The theft and murder had happened almost equidistant between them. Kyle wondered, standing on what was nearly the spot where Corinne died—though he could not be sure it was the exact spot—how capricious life and death really are. Someone who lives through sixty years of life's calamities suddenly loses his life in a traffic accident he would have avoided had the car arrived at the point of impact five seconds earlier or later. A woman boards an airplane that plummets to earth just as it arcs toward the sun, while another woman misses the flight, often crediting God with her safety without ever wondering what God had against the people on board.

Kyle had gone over the police reports several times at his desk. The details were permanently sketchy, with only two witnesses, neither of whom saw the killer's face. He'd been wearing a hoodie, the modern version of a ski mask and so ubiquitous it worked to criminals' advantage: everybody notices a man in a ski mask, but nowadays people of all ages, sexes, professions and genders thought nothing of walking with their faces hidden.

He'd been short, they said, no taller than the girl he shot. Or maybe he was slumped down, or maybe it was a trick of the early evening light as shadows unique to tall buildings dimmed the streets on the brightest of days. They'd heard an argument and thought it might be a lover's quarrel. Then one gunshot. Was it a gunshot? And the man in the dark red hoodie (or was it blue, or green?) ran back along 37th toward Eighth. The two witnesses realized the woman, who they only later knew was a seventeen-year-old girl, had fallen to the pavement. One ran to her and called 911; the other stood transfixed, looking up the street to see if the man was coming back.

The witnesses: a woman named Eileen McDermott, who lived In an apartment on 37th Street, close to Tenth Avenue. She'd worked a little late and was walking home from her job in Chelsea. Forty-two years old. A bookkeeper. Eileen had been on the other side of the street, the north side, and was almost at Ninth Avenue when she heard the woman shouting. She'd turned around, heard the shot, seen the man fleeing, and run to the fallen girl. Eileen is the one who stayed with Corinne as the life flowed out of her skull in a bloodstain. Eileen who waited for the ambulance. Eileen who gave a statement to the police, then another to Detective Robin Dietz, and one — only one — to a reporter from the New York Times. She did not use the tragedy for a moment of fame. In fact, she disappeared from public view very quickly after the shooting. She didn't like the attention, she said, and she didn't like reporters showing up outside her apartment building acting as if they cared when all they wanted was more copy.

The second witness was a man named Javier Vasquez who owned a pretzel and hot dog vending cart. He parked it at the corner of 37th Street and Eighth Avenue and had been wheeling it back to his car when the murder occurred. Javier was a naturalized citizen from Chihuahua, Mexico, who'd been in the United States for fifteen years. Like many immigrants he feared repercussions, even though he could not be deported. It was a fact of life for people in his community; some of them were undocumented, including his brother Reynaldo, and Javier would just as soon have no involvement with the authorities. But Javier was a good man, and Javier had witnessed the killing of a teenager — a child — so Javier had done the right thing, stayed at the scene, and given a statement. It offered nothing more helpful than Eileen's statement, so the police had spoken to him once and let it go.

Kyle was frustrated at the lack of hard evidence to go on. Both witnesses, along with a half dozen others in the area, shop owners, even Niz Ramani at the 38-Nine Deli, had all been questioned, some repeatedly. It had happened so fast; it was as if they'd dreamed it, and the dream became a nightmare for Detective Dietz, the NYPD, and the city itself. What was the world coming to, that a young girl would be murdered for a phone? Was anyone safe?

The third anniversary of the murde" was'just a week away. It gave the whole matter a strange sense of having happened recently when it was, as murders go, very cold. It also added urgency to Kyle's quest. He thought, however irrationally, that if he did not solve this thing, or at least come up with new leads the police could follow, that it would never be solved. Standing there on that sidewalk was like looking at a window quickly closing. Each day it would close a little more, and finally, on April 23rd when the anniversary came and went, no one would ever be able to open it again. That's what he thought, what he *felt*.

He considered going storefront-to-storefront, asking questions that had been asked three years go. There was a television repair store just up the street, with the kinds of old televisions in the window no one owned anymore. There was a barbershop practically in front of the spot where Corinne was killed. Had it been there then? Had it been open, and how could people in a barbershop with a murder being committed just beyond its window not have seen it? Kyle guessed it wasn't there three years ago. Such was the fleeting nature of business in a city where most ended quickly. He considered walking up and down 37th Street, back and forth, two times, three times, trying to get some sudden insight, but he knew it would be for nothing. Insight would not come this afternoon. And he had Imogene to think of, too. She'd be back soon from chasing quotes on the Raul Sandoval story. She'd expect Kyle to be in his cubicle, ready to serve in any capacity she needed. He'd done enough for now. He would take the envelope home, with its news clippings, official reports, and the sad journal from Skate Copley, and he would sit quietly with it at his desk.

Speak to me, he said, whispering the words. *I'm listening, Corinne. Just speak to me.*

He sighed, shoved his hands in his pants pockets, and walked slowly back to work.

CHAPTER Nine

Much had changed in their lives the last nine months. Margaret Bowman, the founder and owner of famed Gramercy Park restaurant Margaret's Passion, had first sold the restaurant to Danny, Kyle and Kyle's mother Sally, then given the building it was in to Danny and Kyle just before moving to Florida. She was in her eighties now and wanted to spend her remaining years with her sister Rebecca in Coral Springs. Kyle and Danny had already been to visit her once and were planning to go again at Christmas.

They'd bought out Kyle's mother in an effort to keep the family peace (Sally Callahan had not been the silent partner Danny envisioned when they borrowed money from her to secure the deal, despite living in Chicago). It worked, once Sally's wounded pride healed, which had taken blessedly little time. And now the men were not only restaurateurs—or, rather, Danny was, since Kyle left everything to do with owning and running Margaret's Passion up to his husband—they were landlords as well. Following Margaret's advice, they'd retained the management company that had acted as her de facto landlords for twenty years. The restaurant was on the ground floor, and Margaret's apartment, the one above the restaurant, where she and her late husband Gerard had lived for thirty-five years, had been renovated and rented several months back. It was not a tall building, having only four stories and sixteen tenants, but the management company handled all that for them and Kyle and Danny were rarely called upon to deal with problems in the building. Most of their tenants had been in their apartments for decades; while it made for minimal income (the building was rent stabilized), it also made for very few headaches.

Kyle's work life had thankfully not changed. There was a time, between the murders surrounding the Katherine Pride Gallery and the climactic, devastating end of the Pride Killer's long run, when Kyle had worried his boss Imogene would take another job. She'd become a minor celebrity, first for the late-late-night Tokyo audience who found the diminutive loudmouth amusing, then for New Yorkers who'd been clued into this entertaining C-list news reporter, and finally to station heads in markets around the country. Kyle had been certain she would move on to Seattle or Boston or even Los Angeles, but Imogene had proven that her loyalty to New York and to Kyle was stronger than any pull of fame. He thought age might have something to do with it; they were all in their fifties, and Imogene, among the least naïve people Kyle had ever met, knew the odds were against her in a job market where looks were prized above most attributes. She was a star right where she was, and she had no desire to risk losing her sheen or her job in an often cruel and heartless business.

His second-best friend Linda Sikorsky had seen her life change as well. Married, living in her little house in the woods, running her store, *For Pete's Sake* and, from what she told Kyle on a regular basis, enjoying the best years of her life. She'd loved being a cop—a homicide detective at that—but all things pass; the key to staying engaged in life was knowing when to let them. Her career on the police force had run its course. And now she was a wife and a business owner, married to a woman who had also made a major change. Changes were unavoidable if you simply lived long enough.

Kyle was sitting on the living room couch, the contents of Skate Copley's envelope in neat piles on the coffee table. The television was on but muted; Kyle looked up every now and then to see some America's Next Top Something Talent Competition playing out on the screen years after it should have taken its dignity and moved to an assisted living facility.

Danny came in and sat on the couch, trailed by Smelly and Leonard. He'd expected Kyle to join him in the bedroom an hour ago. That's where the couple spent most of their evenings, watching television in bed; sometimes Danny read a magazine while Kyle read a novel or went over scripts for Imogene. But Kyle had stayed in the living room and Danny knew something was different. He'd worried ever since Kyle told him about the Corinne Copley case. Not so much for Kyle's safety — it was likely the case would stay cold and the killer would never be found — but for his well-being. Six-plus months of therapy had changed Kyle in subtle ways. He seemed more brooding now, more melancholy. He did not talk much with Danny about the things that were discussed with his therapist, and that made Danny wonder if he was one of those things they talked about. Their relationship had been solid from the very beginning and there was nothing to be concerned about now, but Danny kept waiting for Kyle to open up about the issues he'd gone to therapy to deal with, and whatever issues he'd discovered there. Patience was the only way he knew to handle it; just wait, and if Kyle ever wanted to discuss the conversations he had with Peter Benoit at home with Danny, he would do that. If not, Danny would accept that absolutely everyone had secrets, and needed them.

"What's up?" Danny asked, sitting on the couch next to Kyle. He looked at the contents of the envelope splayed across the coffee table.

"I don't know where to start," Kyle said, sighing. "That's not true. I do know where to start — at the beginning."

"But you don't know where the beginning is."

"Exactly," said Kyle. He turned and faced Danny. "Everyone assumes this was a random killing. But that means it probably won't ever be solved. Unless the gun used to kill this girl turns up somewhere and they trace it back to that night, on that street. The odds are very slim.

"No, I think it began much earlier than that. Maybe that morning when she left home knowing she was not going to school. Maybe even earlier, when they girls first planned to skip school."

"Is that what happened?" Danny asked.

"Yes. Corinne Copley and her friend Lydia Becker planned for weeks to skip school and go to this restaurant, Constantine—"

"I know it well. It was the hottest ticket in town three years ago. Part of the Oasis Hotel that just opened then."

"Six months earlier, actually," Kyle said. "But yes, that's the place. So the girls head off with their parents thinking they're going to school, but instead they hang out, walk around, and end up at this restaurant for lunch."

"How do you know all this?" Danny asked.

"It's in the statements. Skate had copies of all of it—police reports, witness statements, even the coroner's report. That's how they knew about the restaurant. I mean, Lydia told them, too, but they confirmed where she'd been from her stomach contents."

"Jesus."

"Yeah, pretty harsh stuff for a father to read."

"And where did a father get all this? They don't usually make these things public."

"He got them from this detective in the Seventeenth Precinct. They cover Hell's Kitchen. I have a feeling this detective, Robin Dietz is his name, was feeding information to Skate when the case officially went cold. He's another person I have to talk to."

Danny looked at Kyle. He didn't seem the least bit tired.

"I think you should sleep on it," Danny said. "Put it away for now, come to bed. The cats are impatient."

"They just want warm bodies to lie next to," Kyle said. "But sure, I'll be in in a minute. I want to reorganize these papers and make a couple notes."

Kyle started gathering up the sheets of paper and setting them in piles. He would leave them out and revisit them in the morning.

"You know," Kyle said, "if I work backward from the shooting to that morning, or I start that morning and work toward the shooting, it all begins in the same place."

"And where is that?" Danny asked, standing from the couch.

"With two girls heading off on an adventure, something different, something neither of them would normally do. She was close to her father. Her mother, I don't yet know about — they're divorced, by the way — but from what little I've learned and from knowing Skate the last few years at the deli, to listen to him talk, father and daughter were very tight. It wasn't like her not to tell him she was skipping school. It was a secret, and the only other person who knew it was Lydia Becker. That's where I have to start."

"Do you even know where to find her? She's not a teenager anymore. She may not even live in Manhattan now."

"Yes, yes, and she does," Kyle said. "Remember, I find things out about people for a living, when I'm not getting lunch for Imogene."

Kyle finally got up, knowing Danny was not going to leave him in the living room to return to his fixation. He glanced a last time at the papers on the coffee table, then followed Danny into the bedroom, turning off the living room light as the two men, each trailed by a cat, headed to bed for the night.

CHAPTER Ten

Kyle began Thursday morning doing something he had rarely done in seven years working for Imogene Landis—he called in sick. And not only sick, but sick in advance: he sent her an email at five o'clock that morning telling her he would be out the rest of the week. It was only two days, but it was unprecedented. One sick day, sure; maybe a half day if it was a slow news cycle, but two days? She would wonder how he knew he'd be sick Friday as well. She would email him, text him, tweet him and call him, and she would get no response until he was ready to communicate again.

Kyle's relationship with his boss was not complicated. It was very simple, in fact: they loved each other (he could say that after all this time), they relied on each other—Kyle on Imogene to give purpose to his days, and Imogene on Kyle for pretty much everything. She was also indebted to Kyle and not afraid to admit it. The murders he got involved with, and the murderers who committed them, were what made her fading star rise spectacularly again. So calling in sick would annoy her, but not for more than the two days he was out. She would forget about it quickly, especially if he solved this case. Any exclusive would be hers. An interview with Skate Copley? Done. An in-depth profile with Kyle and how he solved a case that had baffled the NYPD? Done. (He could handle the spotlight now, after his experience with the Pride Killer. Before that he'd shied away from the press, but the story had been too big, too important and he'd had no choice. The upside was that it got him accustomed to microphones and sound bites and people nosing around his life. Numb might be more accurate; hardened, too.)

He was back at his desk in the guest room. He'd taken the papers, reports and journal pages from the coffee table and was sitting in front of his computer. It was now nine o'clock and he was waiting for a time that didn't seem too early to call

Lydia Becker. He knew she had not left town. He knew she'd gone to NYU for three years to study International Relations and dropped out after the first semester of this year. He knew her parents were divorced and Lydia lived at home, that she'd always lived at home and commuted to the University by subway. And he knew all this because lives today were very public and accessible. Lydia, like most people now, chronicled her life in photos, comments and status updates on a dizzying variety of social media. It was all there to see—Lydia at dinner with her friends, Lydia at a museum, Lydia at the beach. A daily, running catalog of activities and a timeline of events stretching back to when Lydia was thirteen. But nothing, oddly, of the day Corinne Copley was killed, and that was the only day Kyle was truly interested in. He wanted to talk to her about that day. Some things still required conversation, and he was hoping she would talk to him.

Danny ducked his head into the room, nodded when Kyle looked at him, then ducked back out. He'd been awake when Kyle sent his email to Imogene. He knew to leave well enough alone and not ask Kyle what the repercussions would be of taking two days off during the biggest story of the year. Raul Sandoval had been formally accused of selling his office for favors. He'd professed his innocence with as much preening and indignation as a man can display, and now they would have to wait and see how it played out.

Kyle was online reading about Constantine, the once-red hot restaurant where Corinne Copley ate her last meal, when the door buzzer rang.

Odd, thought Kyle. Maybe the laundry had been delivered, although that came at night.

"Can you get that?" Danny shouted from the bathroom.

"Sure," Kyle shouted back. He got up and headed to the front door. The intercom was on the wall and Kyle pressed the button.

"Yes?" Kyle said, waiting to hear Vinnie's reply.

Vincent Campagna was one of three main doormen who worked on shifts in the building's lobby. It was his brother, Victor, who'd been the first victim of the Pride Killer's last spree, and why Kyle had taken those murders so personally. Vinnie had not left his job after that; he'd not moved away. But it was a topic none of them discussed — ever.

"You've got a visitor," Vinnie's voice said. "Detective Sikorsky."

Vinnie had come to know Linda after she and Kyle first questioned him about his brother's movements the day he was murdered, then throughout the firestorm of press and police investigation. He was never interrogated; he was among the family of the murdered man. But he was questioned several times as the sordid, successful and sadistic career of the Pride Killer was examined from every possible angle and for every lurid detail.

Vinnie knew Linda was retired, and he was the only person besides Kyle and Danny who called her "Detective."

Kyle was startled by the announcement. What was Linda doing here? And why hadn't she told him she was coming?

Because she's worried about you, he thought. It was the truth, and Linda would admit as much, but why not tell him ahead of time? Did she think he would convince her not to come? No one convinced Linda Sikorsky of anything she did not want to be convinced of, with the possible exception of her wife.

"Hello?" Vinnie said. "Can you hear me?"

"I hear you perfectly well," Kyle said. "Send her up, please."

Danny came out of the bathroom brushing his teeth. He was six inches shorter than Kyle, who was not a tall man, and he was wearing the heart-covered pajamas Kyle had given him for Valentine's Day. They'd sent the wrong size; the pant legs bunched up around Danny's feet and threatened to trip Danny whenever he wore them.

"You need to get those taken up," Kyle said, nodding at the pajama bottoms.

Danny knew this. He also liked the way they felt and, for some reason known only to Danny, the fact they were too long. He'd promised a dozen times to take them to the laundry across from their apartment and have the hems stitched up, then each time he'd conveniently forgotten.

"You'll catch me if I fall," Danny said. "Isn't that what marriage is about?"

Kyle smiled. "Just don't take the stairs in those, please. They'll say I pushed you."

"Who's here?" Danny asked through a mouthful of toothpaste.

"Detective Linda."

Danny's eyes shot up. "Did you know she was coming?"

"No," said Kyle, "and I'm sure she wanted it that way."

"She knows you almost as well as I do. She doesn't want you chasing after criminals alone." He'd started to add, "She's got her gun, too," but did not. It was the gun Kyle and Diedrich Keller had been fighting over when it went off, sending a bullet through Keller's heart.

Danny waved and headed back into the bathroom just as the door buzzer sounded.

Kyle took a deep breath. Detective Linda was his dear friend, but she was not his mother. He was wondering how to send her home without hurting her feelings as he opened the door.

"I hope you've got clean sheets on the sofa bed," Linda said, walking into the apartment with a packed gym bag. She was wearing jeans, a gray sweater and a blue windbreaker. Kyle looked at her quickly, checking to see if her shoulder holster was on. He'd become familiar with its bulge beneath her jacket from her last visit. No holster, but that did not mean no gun. It could be in her purse, or she might have a new one strapped to her ankle. He hoped she'd left it at home. Who needs a gun for a cold case, anyway? He was chasing ghosts and tragedy, nothing more.

"I missed your text," he said, closing the apartment door. "The one that said you were coming to the city."

"There wasn't one," she replied.

"Oh, the voicemail then, or the email."

Linda could tell Kyle was annoyed with her sudden appearance. "Listen, Kyle, I didn't tell you because I was coming no matter how persuasive you were in telling me not to."

"I don't need help with this, Detective."

Linda took a seat on the couch as Kyle walked around and sat in the overstuffed chair opposite her.

"You know, you're the one who should be called Detective now, not me. I'm retired a year and a half. Hell, they barely remember me at the station."

"That's an exaggeration," Kyle said. "Nobody forgets Linda Sikorsky. For your height, if nothing else. There aren't too many … statuesque quasi-blonde ex-homicide detectives roaming around New Hope."

"Don't you mean Amazonian? Or maybe just big-boned. That's what my mother calls me."

"You're impossible to miss, and to forget."

"Thank you. I think."

"You want a cup of coffee?" Kyle said. "Since it looks like you're here to stay."

"I'd love one, yes."

Kyle headed into the kitchen. He took a cup from the cabinet and popped a K-cup into the coffee machine.

"What more have you learned from the material he gave you?" Linda said from the living room. She could observe Kyle to her left: Manhattan apartments were never very large, no matter their size. Kitchens flowed into living rooms that flowed into bedrooms, with a bathroom somewhere around a corner.

"Quite a few things," Kyle said. He stirred creamer into her coffee, knowing how she took it, then brought it back and set it on a coaster on the coffee table in front of her.

"I learned his daughter's movements that day. I learned she and her friend Lydia skipped school without telling anyone, and that it was out of character for her."

"Which means they kept it a secret," Linda said.

"Yes, a secret I think plays into this somehow."

Linda reached for her coffee and took a sip. "How so?"

"I don't know yet," said Kyle. "But there's something there. I just … I keep thinking this wasn't random. But everyone, for three years, has assumed it was."

"And that's why it's a cold case."

"Very possibly."

"Or maybe," Linda said, "you want to believe it wasn't random, because then you might find out the truth of it." She waited a moment. "What if there isn't anymore truth to it, Kyle? What if she was just a kid on the wrong street at the wrong time and you're looking for answers that vanished back into the chaos of coincidence?"

"The 'chaos of coincidence.' I like that," said Kyle. "Actually, I don't like it at all. It means we're wasting our time."

Linda smiled at the 'we.' She knew Kyle had already accepted her presence, as well he should — resistance was futile.

"But before you throw anymore cold water on this cold case, Detective, let's suspend our disbelief awhile and operate on the assumption there is something — maybe several things — the others missed. Something we can find."

"Where do we start?" she asked.

"On that day, at the beginning."

"And where would that be?"

"With Lydia Becker."

"The friend."

Kyle had given much of the information to Linda on their Skype call the day before.

"Yes," he said. "The person who was with her that day and the last to see her alive."

"The killer was the last one to see her alive," Linda said.

"You know what I mean. Lydia was the last person who knew her."

"And you know where Lydia can be found?" Linda said. It was a rhetorical question; Kyle would not be bringing it up if he didn't already have the answer.

"What time is it?"

Kyle glanced at the digital clock by the television. It was 10:00 a.m.. Even New Yorkers who slept late were awake up by now. He got up, walked into the kitchen and retrieved his cell phone from the counter where he let it charge at night.

"Let's give Lydia a call," he said. "I'll put her on speaker."

Kyle clicked a button on his phone and the sound of a dial tone could be heard, followed by the beeps and blurts of a phone number.

"You know her number already?" Linda asked.

"I memorized it this morning, when you were on your way here without telling me."

They could hear a ringing on the other end. Twice, three times. Kyle was afraid it would go to voicemail when the sound of a woman's voice came over the phone.

"Hello?" she said. There was no way to gauge her age. She could be twenty, she could be forty.

Kyle glanced at Linda, then said into the phone, "Hi. I'm looking for Lydia Becker."

"This is she."

"Lydia," Kyle said, "my name's Kyle Callahan. I'm a friend of Corinne Copley's father."

There was silence on the line. Kyle hoped she was not about to hang up.

"That was a long time ago," Lydia said.

Kyle had the urge to tell her three years was not such a long time. Instead, he said, "I know, and I'm sorry to disturb you, but I was wondering if we could talk."

"We are talking."

There was a coolness to her voice. He had to choose his words carefully.

"I know you've been over this many times," Kyle said gently. "I just want to take one more look at it—for Skate."

He hoped mentioning Skate's name would help, and maybe even play on Lydia's conscience. Everyone knew about Skate's fall from the heights; Lydia would be especially aware of it.

"I don't think there's much I can tell," she said. "And nothing I haven't said before."

"Hello," Linda said into the phone, startling Kyle. "My name's Linda Sikorsky. I'm a retired detective and a friend of Kyle's. We just want to help Corinne's father—to try one last time. Just a few minutes in person, that's all we need."

Perhaps it was hearing a woman's voice that touched Lydia, or the repeated mention of Corinne's father.

"There's a coffee shop at Fifty-Seventh and Seventh, called Beantown."

"I know it," Kyle said.

"I'll be there in an hour."

"So will we," said Linda. "And thank you so much for this, Lydia. We promise you won't get dragged into anything."

"I'd be fine if I did," Lydia replied, surprising them both. "I'd like nothing more than to see the sonofabitch who killed Corinne rot in prison."

"Thank you, again," said Kyle. "See you in an hour."

He hung up. They had some time before they had to leave for the coffee shop and Kyle wanted to spend it going over the clippings and reports. He'd pay for a taxi to get them to Beantown in fifteen minutes. Until then they had work to do.

CHAPTER Eleven

Beantown Coffee had survived the onslaught of Starbucks and the other chain coffee shops that now dominated Manhattan. It helped that there was only one. Another factor in its favor was its location: a block from Carnegie Hall, on a corner that fed it a steady stream of commuters flowing into and out of the subways. Morning coffee, lunchtime coffee, after work coffee. The world, or at least New York City, ran on caffeine. It fueled all the pedestrians rushing frantically to nowhere, zigging and zagging their way around each other while having their faces down, their eyes glued to smartphones and tablets. Almost like bats, Kyle thought as he and Linda exited from a taxi at 57th and Seventh. (One dispensed with the words "Street" and "Avenue" in Manhattan. Coordinates were given in number combinations: 57th and Seventh, Ninth and 32nd.)

Kyle was unusually conscientious when he walked around the city; he stopped if he needed to use his phone, stepped to the side out of foot traffic, and took care of the moment's business without being a nuisance or a danger to anyone else. It wasn't behavior he saw in others, who, if they stopped at all, stopped in the middle of the sidewalk and sometimes even in the middle of the street, texting or typing or reading as if their full attention was demanded at that very moment. At every moment, anywhere they were with a phone and a pair of opposable thumbs.

Linda looked up at the entrance to Beantown. It stood on the corner, with high windows lining each side. The interior was large and could be seen in its entirety from outside, with tables and stools spread around, quite a few of them occupied at 11:00 a.m. on a Thursday morning. She got to the door first and held it for Kyle.

Once they entered, the smell of muffins, scones and breakfast sandwiches filled their nostrils.

"I'm hungry," Linda said as they stood inside the door looking around.

"That's the point," said Kyle. "They want you to be hungry and thirsty."

Kyle glanced at a table in back and saw a young woman looking at them. The curiosity on her face said: is that you? He nodded, then waved. Lydia Becker smiled and waved back.

A moment later they were sitting at the table across from Lydia. She was pretty in a no-frills way. She would be twenty now, an adult, and guessing from what Kyle knew of her experience since Corinne's murder—the murder itself, her parents' divorce, attending college in the city—she'd aged quite a bit. She was wearing jeans and a gray sweater, with a small gold crucifix around her neck.

"Thank you so much for meeting with us," Kyle said.

Lydia shrugged. She had her hands wrapped around a coffee mug, as if she were cold and trying to warm up by the heat of the porcelain.

A waiter wearing a long brown apron came over with two menus. Kyle quickly asked for two cheese croissants with cappuccinos. The waiter said, "Right away," and glided off.

"I don't really know what I can tell you," Lydia said. "And I don't know what you already know."

Kyle waited a moment, then said, "I know what Skate Copley has told me. And he gave me a stack of newspaper items and reports, some writing he did about it."

"Writing? Like a memoir or something?"

"No, not that at all. Just his thoughts, like a journal."

"I imagine that was dark reading," she said. "It ruined his life, you know."

Kyle said nothing. He did not want to assume that just because Skate had gone from being materially successful to working in a deli meant that his life had been ruined. Maybe he liked it this way.

"We thought we would retrace Corinne's steps," Linda said. "Your steps that day."

"It's been done," Lydia said. "Several times."

"There may be something everybody missed," said Kyle.

"That's what you're hoping."

"Yes."

"Because if nobody missed anything, you'll come up as empty-handed as everyone else has."

She was right and they both knew it. But Kyle had to try. He'd already felt himself forgetting the depression and the confusion of the last nine months. Not quite moving past it, but having his attention focused on the here and now, not on a deadly afternoon in a killer's basement.

The waiter returned with a tray, quickly setting two small plates in front of them, each holding a croissant, and two cappuccinos. Kyle thanked him and he vanished again.

"I keep thinking," Kyle said, "that somewhere along the way that day Corinne caught this man's attention. The man who shot her."

"She did," Lydia replied. "On Thirty-Seventh Street, at approximately six-thirty that night."

"He means before that," Linda said. "Before she even got to that street."

"Maybe at a store she stopped in, or at the movies. We know she went to a movie."

"That's my fault," Lydia said, looking down at her hands.

"Nothing was your fault," said Linda

"It doesn't feel that way. I've thought for three years that if I'd stayed with Corinne, if I hadn't been petulant and gone home after that lunch—I wasn't supposed to, you know. I was supposed to stay with her for the day, until, well ..."

The "well" would be when Corinne found a way to ditch Lydia for the dinner party with her friend Gilda and their teenage cohort that did not include Lydia.

"You weren't at fault in any way," Linda said.

"I try to think that," said Lydia. "So what can I tell you?"

"Just start by recalling that day," said Kyle. "From the beginning."

April 23rd, morning. Every New Yorker's favorite time of year, unless you prefer the gaudy excesses of Christmas or the coming of autumn to Central Park. Summer is out — nobody loves summers in Manhattan, or Brooklyn, or Queens. Summer stinks of leaking trash bags and open-air urinals. Summer pushes down on you with unrelenting heat and a stifling wetness to the air. But spring? April? Dry, cool, clear air. Blue sky. To be in it is to feel renewed, to feel alive, walking down the street with a bounce in your step and a breeze blowing by you. There's nothing like it, and that's how it had been that day three years ago. Corinne Copley was already thinking of the party that night at Maria's Cantina. She'd been invited to celebrate her best friend Gilda's Birthday. Gilda, like Corinne, was an only child, with parents who could afford a large co-op on Christopher Street. Corinne had been there many times, just as Gilda had often been to the Copley's apartment on Central Park South. The girls had been inseparable since third grade when they'd both attended PS 41 in Greenwich Village. The Copleys had moved since then but they remained as close as friends could be, and it was Gilda, with a handful of others who maintained constant contact through Facebook, Twitter, Instagram and texting, that Corinne was planning to meet for dinner that night.

Her second-best friend was Lydia, and that's who she was skipping school with that day. Corrine was at that age when teenagers can be cruelest, but she tried to watch herself, to check her snark and her snaps and the putdowns that came too easily to a girl like herself — smart, pretty, vivacious, popular. It was easy for teenagers like Corinne to become insensitive, surrounded either by those who were like them, or those who wanted to be them. For, you see, Corinne was also very perceptive, not a trait often used to describe her peers. She was aware of her good fortune. She was aware of her advantages. And she was aware how these things could turn her into someone she didn't like. Someone like Sylvia Montoya or Gregg Capella. Not-nice kids who erected pedestals for themselves and stood on them looking down at the rest of humanity. Corinne was determined not to be one of them. So she was friends with Lydia and several others considered outside her circle, if not beneath it. Lydia was a good girl. They had that in common. The closest they came to being outlaws was cutting class, which they'd done that day. A new hotel had opened in Midtown and word quickly spread that the upper echelon of popular culture was dining at Constantine, the hotel's flagship restaurant. Household names, sliding into and out of limousines. Star couples rumored to be divorcing or sleeping with gay lovers. So on that day Corinne and Lydia said they were going to school, then detoured separately to meet at a bakery in the Village. Lunch would not be for several more hours and they had time to kill.

The only drawback to skipping school was that Corinne could not put their adventure on her Facebook page. She couldn't upload her photos to Instagram, or tweet that she'd seen Taylor Swift being spirited into a gold Escalade (if Taylor was there, as Corinne and Lydia hoped). Her parents, especially her father, had the annoying habit of following her on every social media she joined. It wasn't quite creepy — she did not consider her dad a stalker — but it inhibited her in some ways. She suspected that was his motive. He wanted her to be careful; he warned her many times of the inherent dangers of the internet, whether from online predators or future college admissions departments or employers who looked to see what sort of person was applying for jobs with them.

"Nothing ever goes away online," Skate had repeatedly told her. "Look what happened to So-and-So, she posted pictures from a frat party and never worked again." Or, "Remember Stefan, last year's valedictorian? One picture of himself with a beer hose down his throat and bye-bye Harvard." Something like that. Many things like that. Skate Copley was not so much a helicopter parent as an ever-vigilant one. Corinne loved him and her mother, too, but sometimes their caution could be stifling. Sometimes it forced Corinne to be clandestine. This day it meant her daring-do with Lydia, their naughty expedition, had to be secret. She took some solace in that. She was a very, very good girl, and doing something like this was both outside her normal behavior and quite exciting.

Oasis had opened in November of the previous year to enormous publicity. Promoted as the future of the high-end hospitality industry, it had its own premiere party, complete with stars from the music and art worlds, high financiers, sports figures who hadn't yet fallen from grace, and the publishing industry. A reporter from the New York Times was there and the write-up in that weekend's magazine only cemented Oasis's sudden reputation as the place to stay, dance, be seen, and eat. It boasted two restaurants, each overseen by celebrity chefs. One of the two, Constantine, named for its head chef Constantine Anastas, was where Corinne and Lydia went for lunch her last day on Earth. It was well known that you might find yourself at a table across from Bradley Cooper or Viola Davis, if either was in town. It was also insanely expensive, and the two girls had saved portions of their allowances for the past two months to eat there.

They could have waited till the weekend. They should have waited till the weekend. But that would have taken the naughtiness out of it, the thrill. It also would have made everything turn out differently. Corinne would still be alive. Skate would still be living his previous dream, the one with the wife and daughter and apartment on Central Park South with a terrace overlooking the park. The darkness that came over their lives – in Corinne's case ultimate and permanent – would still be waiting far in the distance where lives dim naturally. They did not wait for the weekend. They met after leaving for school on a Tuesday morning with nothing but fun in mind, captured in cellphone photos Corinne could not share, at least not until she confessed to her parents, which she planned to do in a couple days when the element of rebellion would not seem so strong. It was a harmless teenage escape that turned everything upside down and smashed it into dust.

Lydia finished telling them the story of that day, how they'd met that morning at L'Italia Bakery on Bleecker Street, how they'd been disappointed with Constantine, how the expense had been more than Lydia had anticipated and Corinne had made up the difference.

"It was embarrassing," Lydia said. "I took fifty dollars with me, you'd think that could cover a lunch anywhere, but this wasn't just anywhere. It was *the* place eat then. Or to be seen, at least. But everybody worth seeing had moved on."

She still had her hands wrapped around her coffee cup. It was empty now and could not still be warm.

"We stopped on the way to the subway so Corinne could take pictures of us in front of some apartment building. I don't know why, she said famous people lived there."

"Did you take pictures, too?" Linda asked.

"I didn't see the point," Lydia said. "We couldn't put them on Facebook, couldn't tweet, couldn't Instagram, none of it."

"Why is that?" asked Kyle.

"Because nobody knew we were skipping school!" Lydia said, as if it were obvious. "Our parents saw everything, especially Corinne's dad. He friended her, followed her, kept an eye her. He'd know we weren't at school the minute she posted a photo. She took them anyway, since she'd confess soon enough, I knew she would, and then I'd have to, but we just wanted a fun day to ourselves. So no, I didn't take pictures, Corinne did. Then we walked to the subway. I can still see her standing there, waving at me when I went down the stairs. I looked back, waved, and that was the last time I ever saw her."

She'd been right — there was nothing new to tell them. But Kyle believed, because he had to, that along their path, along Corinne's path after Lydia went down into the subway, they would find a scrap, a key, a missing piece.

"I have to go now," Lydia said, freeing one hand to look at her watch. "I'm meeting my mother for lunch. That's why I didn't eat anything here. Plus it's not very good."

Linda would have to agree. The croissant had been cold and the cappuccino tasted like any cappuccino from any coffee shop.

"So you met for the day at L'Italia Bakery," Kyle said, repeating what Lydia had told them.

"Yes, that's where it all started. The son of the owner is a lech, if you can be a lech at thirty or whatever he is. Joey DeCresce. He had a thing for Corinne."

"A thing?" said Linda.

"A stalker thing."

Linda and Kyle looked at each other.

"We went there on Saturdays sometimes," Lydia explained. "Joey was there. He's always there. And once he saw Corinne the first time, it's like he couldn't take his eyes off her. And not in a way girls want to be looked at."

"Is that all he did?" Kyle asked. "Stare at her?"

"It was enough. He stared at her in the bakery. He stared at her on Facebook. He followed her on Twitter. It went on for a few months."

Lydia could tell what they were thinking. "But he was interrogated — interviewed, whatever — and he wasn't anywhere near Corinne when she was killed. It was on the news. Every sordid bit. They even talked about Skate and Jennifer like they were bad parents. Really upsetting."

Kyle listened politely and did not dispute anything Lydia told them, but he would decide for himself if Joey DeCresce had been nowhere near 37th Street that night and not in any way involved. He had no reason at this point to doubt what others had discovered in their investigations, but L'Italia Bakery was a good place to start.

"You can get the subway near here to Christopher Street if you want to. It's a short walk from there to the bakery."

"We'll do that," Linda said, "and thank you so much again."

Lydia slid out of her chair, opening her purse on the table.

"We'll get this," said Kyle.

"Thanks," she said, and with a small wave she left them, hurrying out and around the corner.

"So," Kyle said. "Are you ready for another croissant? A good one? I've heard about L'Italia. It's been there forever, supposed to be amazing."

"Are we going to be eating our way through the day? I should know ahead of time."

"Only if it's helpful," Kyle said, meaning only if it helped them engage people in conversation. They had questions to ask of people who had been asked them before, and if buying a cannoli or a sandwich kept the conversation going, then they'd have to just accept it.

"We can always nibble," Kyle said.

He put a twenty dollar bill on the table, waited a moment for Linda to stand, then led them out.

Several minutes later they were descending into the subway. A train could be heard pulling into the station. Kyle told Linda to hurry and picked up his pace, not wanting to wait for the next one.

Part II

The Company One Keeps

CHAPTER Twelve

Raul was exhausted. He'd been in front of cameras many times, but not as an indicted suspect in one of the biggest political scandals to ever rock Manhattan. It had never been hard for him to keep up an appearance of bluster. For Raul it wasn't an act; he'd been blustering, flourishing and barreling his way through life since he was a hardscrabble kid in the Bronx living a hardscrabble life. You didn't get through that existence being sheepish, and Raul was not the sheep—he was the wolf. Until now.

Raul had graduated the top of his class at Harvard Law while his brothers made little or nothing of themselves. He'd supported his parents until his father died, then taken care of his mother after that. She was in a nursing home now in Westchester with early-onset Alzheimer's, but it was one of the best facilities in the state. A place like that cost a lot of money. An apartment like the one Raul lived in on the twelfth floor of the Centurion cost a lot of money. His wife Gloria and his two daughters, both in college, cost a lot of money. Money, money, money. What was he supposed to do? His father, Alejandro, had been adamant about not incurring debt. Respectable men owed no one. Men of honor did not indebt themselves to banks or department stores or doctors, and most of all not to men of dishonor. Raul had taken his father's advice and lived by it—with the exception of the part about dishonorable men. There was no way to avoid them, in politics or in business. Raul had needed cash at various times in his life and there had always been someone willing to provide it for a significant rate of interest in either money or favors. As Raul discovered, favors were much harder to hide than money.

He had risen slowly but steadily in New York City politics and political circles. He had started at the bottom, running for office, such as it was, at his daughter Reina's grammar school.

He gained a seat on the school advisory board, and it was all an upward trajectory from there. School council, one committee after the other, then, degree in hand, a spot at the Manhattan District Attorney's office. Ten years later he was the first Hispanic District Attorney the borough had ever had, and he was big news. Profiled in *New York Magazine*, interviewed on Univision, he'd even been slated for the cover of *Time* until that damn Obama managed to put a bullet in Osama bin Laden's head. Timing, as Raul well knew, was everything, and it had turned on him with a vengeance.

There were certain people of means—some of it ill-gotten—who had needed favors from Raul over the years. He'd granted them for a price. He'd always known it was a dangerous game, but, like all men with egos the size of Raul's, he thought he could beat the odds, that he could keep his shadowy dealings away from the light. He was that smart, that clever, that careful. But someone, somewhere, was bound to slip up. Someone was bound to be arrested for something, then cut a deal in exchange for heads on stakes. That's exactly what happened, and it was now Raul's head that bitch Eleanor Duvall wanted displayed on the castle wall.

He would beat this, he was sure of it. He had to. The more it looked like Raul Sandoval might be the one cutting a deal, the more his life was in danger. There were people who would do everything they could to make sure Raul did not take them down with him. People who killed as easily as everyone else ate breakfast. One in particular who may already be arranging his death. His deal with her had been a deal with the Devil, that was certain, but the Devil made mistakes, too. She had given Raul the phone. Not because he'd wanted it, but because she was arrogant. It was a trophy of sorts. She was saying, "See, Raul Sandoval, there is nothing I cannot do, and this I have done for you." The debt would be his largest ever: cross her and he would die. She might even kill his entire family for good measure. She was known to do that.

The phone was his insurance. He knew it; she knew it. It was probably why they had not yet found him with his throat cut. As long as he had the girl's phone he had a bargaining chip.

She was watching him, he was sure of it. She was enjoying her espresso while she listened to the television news reports about the great Raul Sandoval teetering on the edge of ruin. She had not contacted him for two years, but she would, he knew that. She would want the phone back before the police showed up at his apartment with a search warrant and found it.

He turned at the sound of Gloria entering the apartment. She'd been shopping again. Her husband was being indicted for crimes that could destroy everything they had and put him behind bars until his grandchildren — the ones his daughters would give him — were in high school. Yet she shopped. Gloria believed him when he told her there was nothing to these charges, that this was all a vendetta, a racist campaign to stop him and end his aspirations toward the Governor's mansion. He knew she also chose not to care too much. The money was still there, the apartment, the daughters. He sometimes suspected Gloria made her own arrangements, her own backup plan, but she played dumb. She was so good at it he had never really determined how smart she was.

"So glad you're home," he said, kissing Gloria on the check as she set her large, full and costly shopping bags on the dining room table.

"So glad to be home!" she said. "Shopping exhausts me, I must have walked ten thousand steps in Macy's alone. You're still tracking your steps, aren't you?"

"Always," he said, waving his wristband at her, the one that calculated his steps and heart rate. Its charged had died months ago but he kept it on, knowing she'd ask.

"Do we still have a reservation at Epiphany? I hope so, Sweetheart, it's so hard to get in there."

"Yes, we still have a reservation," he said. "And even if we didn't we would get the best table. I'm Raul Sandoval, remember."

She smiled at him. "I will never forget, my love. Not for a moment."

She set about taking her purchases out of the bags and laying them on the table to look at them again. Raul turned away, not wanting to see the price tags.

Everything in his life had cost so much money, for such a long time.

CHAPTER Thirteen

L'Italia Bakery had occupied the same storefront on Bleecker Street where its founder, Anthony DeCresce, had started his business forty-five years ago. His son, Anthony Jr., took it over when Old Man Tony died, and now, as he was nearing retirement himself, he was passing it on to his favored son Joey. Not because he thought Joey was a great businessman and would keep things running for another generation or two, but because Joey was the least unsavory of his three sons and the least stupid. James DeCresce, son number one, operated a food truck and was on his third wife, while Mark, the youngest, was doing time in Rikers for selling heroin. Only Joey had stayed out of trouble and close to his father's side. It had saved him, Tony believed, but it had also left his father with no better choice.

Kyle and Linda arrived at the bakery close to twelve-thirty, lunch time for people in the area and tourists alike. The place was busy, with a line of customers getting espresso, cappuccinos, pastries, and — new on the menu! — paninis. The sandwiches were Joey's idea; Tony had acquiesced because they could be made with an old waffle iron he picked up at a flea market for two dollars.

Tony was behind the cash register. One surly young woman was helping sell pastries and coffee, and a man they assumed to be Joey was making sandwiches. There were only four small round iron tables in the shop. Most people who came here took their purchases and left.

Kyle eyed the pastry case. Nothing in it looked unique, certainly not amazing, and he wondered if the place survived on nostalgia and falsified Yelp reviews.

"Can I help you?" the woman asked when Kyle and Linda got to the head of the line. She was very thin, with her hair in a long ponytail and a glazed expression developed after waiting on people for most of her adult life.

"I was hoping to speak to Joey," Kyle said.

"Hey Joey!" the woman shouted, without asking why they wanted to talk to him.

Joey glanced over, disinterested. He finished wrapping a panini, walked over, handed it to his father, and turned his attention to Kyle. But first he looked Linda over, waist to head.

He's a lech. Lydia was right, Kyle thought. Lecherous and not very smart. The woman he was ogling was not just a lesbian, but an ex-cop and very comfortable with a gun.

"What can I do for you?" Joey asked, wiping his hands on a stained greasy apron.

Kyle smiled, hoping it was disarming. "We wanted to talk to you about Corinne Copley."

Joey may not be too smart, but he knew not to pretend he didn't know who Corinne Copley was—or had been. Everyone in New York City knew the name. He'd been asked about her many times, casually and not-so-casually. He'd been all but accused of killing her by that prick, Detective Robin Dietz. It had been awhile since then and his anger had cooled to resentment, but he was still unhappy to have two strangers show up in his bakery—it would be his soon, the old man had promised—and his stare moved from Linda's breasts to Kyle's feigned smile.

"I've already said everything I have to say," Joey said.

"We're not here to bother you," Linda said, leaning forward slightly so Joey could get a better look at her cleavage.

"That's right," Kyle added. "We're just doing a story on it as a cold case. I work in television."

That got Joey's attention. Television? Cameras? It could be good for business; traffic wasn't what it used to be and any publicity could help, as long as it was good publicity and no handcuffs were involved.

"What kind of television?" Joey asked. He quickly added, "Let's go in the back where we can talk."

He started to lead them behind the counter to a small back room.

"We got customers!" Tony said.

"Delores can cover me," Joey called back. "Give me ten minutes, Pops, these are TV folks."

Delores quickly eyed them, fussing with her hair, wishing she'd worn something more flattering that day.

Tony shrugged. There was nothing he could do, so instead he snapped his fingers to get Delores's attention and the two of them continued helping customers.

The back room was barely big enough for three people. There was a desk piled with invoices and receipts, a calculator, jars of pens and pencils. Two filing cabinets took up one wall, and there was only one chair.

"Please," Joey said to Linda, motioning to the chair, "for the lady."

Linda sat down while the men stood. Joey closed the door behind them, and suddenly Kyle felt claustrophobic. He could turn around in the small room if he had to, but barely.

"So what channel?" Joey asked.

Realizing Joey was talking to him, Kyle said, "Japan TV3."

"*Japan*?" Joey said. "Like, *Japanese*?"

Kyle waited a moment, then said, "Imogene Landis is my boss."

Joey recognized the name. "That crazy chick? The one who covered all those murders?" It only took Joey a few seconds to realize who Kyle worked for. "I didn't ask your names, sorry, it's busy out there."

Kyle extended his hand. "I'm Kyle Callahan, and this is Linda Sikorsky."

"Oh my fucking God, you killed that serial killer, I know you. Well, I mean, I know who you are."

The possibility of fame suddenly became more real to Joey. He was in the presence of a man who had made headlines across the country, maybe around the world.

"What does Corinne's death have to do with any of it?" Joey said.

"Nothing," said Kyle. "Like I said, we're doing a story on it as a cold case and we thought ..."

"I knew her, sure. She and that Lydia girl came in here sometimes. And they were here that day. But I worked all day, went upstairs for a nap—we live on the third floor of this building, have all my life—then came back until ten that night. It's been said, like, a hundred times."

"Did you notice anyone suspicious?" Linda asked.

"Suspicious? Like how?"

"Maybe following the girls, or staring at them?"

Joey thought about it. "Nobody," he said. "The place was quiet that morning. They got some scones and coffee, had them at a table and left."

"And you never saw them again," Kyle said.

"Not until ... well ... it was on the news that night. The shooting. I was, like, holy fuck. They were in the shop that morning, and now she's dead."

"Corinne," said Kyle.

Joey detected something in Kyle's tone. "Yeah, Corinne, the one who got killed."

"The one you had a thing for."

"Hey!" Joey said. "Hey, what's this really about? I didn't have a thing for her, I just thought she was hot."

"She was seventeen," Linda said. "How old are you, Joey? Thirty? Thirty-five?"

Joey felt trapped in the tiny room. "I think you need to go now," he said, opening the door.

"Her friend said you stalked Corinne," Kyle said. "On social media, maybe hung out outside her apartment."

"She's lying. I never did none of that. I was just friendly, that's all. Is this some kind of Catch a Predator shit? You wearing a wire?"

"You've watched too much television," Kyle said. "We're not here to accuse you of anything, just to follow the girls' footsteps that day, and they started here."

"Yeah, well," said Joey, "they started here and they left, like you two need to do."

Kyle led Linda out of the back office. He saw Delores and Tony, now alone in the shop, staring at them.

"Thanks for your time," Kyle said to them, immediately feeling foolish. They hadn't given him any of their time.

"No thanks for yours," Joey said, ushering them out from behind the counter. "We probably lost some customers just now, they expect to see me. They don't see me, they go somewhere else."

He's as vain as he is unintelligent, Kyle thought. He waved a last time and led Linda out onto the street.

"What do you call a dead end at the beginning?" Linda asked. The visit to L'Italia Bakery had got them nowhere.

"A start," Kyle said. "That's what I call it. A first step."

"What's our second?"

"Constantine," said Kyle, referring to the restaurant where the girls had lunch that day.

"Who are we going to question there, and what questions are we going to ask?"

"Anyone who'll talk to us," Kyle said, leading Linda up the street. "I'll figure out the questions on the way."

They headed to the subway. It would be Linda's second trip underground that day. She didn't like the subway; it made her feel submerged in concrete and noise. But she'd come here for this and she would take a subway, a bus, a taxi, anything she needed to do to help Kyle. She had serious doubts it would end with the case any less cold than when they'd started, but she knew it was breathing new life into her friend, and that's what mattered. He'd been on the brink of something terrible. She was here to bring him back.

CHAPTER Fourteen

Four hours pass quickly when you're seventeen, roaming narrow streets and stopping every few doors to look in the windows of countless boutiques. Lydia had been worried they wouldn't have enough to do after leaving L'Italia, but the next thing she knew they'd killed the time and were almost late for their reservation at Constantine — a mistake that could cost them the table. Stragglers were considered unworthy. You got a ten minute grace period, then your table was given to someone else. Everybody wanted to eat there, and the restaurant had turned away big names, huge names, faces familiar to anyone who ever stood in a grocery store line looking at magazine covers. Show up on time or move on to some lesser establishment where has-beens and wannabes went to be seen by bus boys. So it was to both girls' great relief when the taxi dropped them off in front of the hotel with two minutes to spare.

Oasis had been built midway through the Great Recession. 2008 had seen America brought to its economic knees, and the developers who envisioned a revolution in hotel building sold the idea for Oasis to city planners in part as an act of defiance and renewal: See, Great Recession, we stand tall despite you! We build, we hire, we invest, we invigorate. They chose the corner of West Broadway and Broome Street, just about halfway between SoHo and Tribeca, to make their grand statement. At eighteen stories, Oasis was by no means the tallest building in Manhattan, or even in the neighborhood where it stood, but it was what was inside the hotel that made it special. The top three floors were luxury condominiums with price tags that could only be paid by the richest of the rich. The ten floors below them were made up of hotel rooms; but this was no Holiday Inn. Many of the rooms were one- or two-bedroom suites, and the "standard" rooms featured whirlpools in the bathrooms, king-sized beds and 75-inch television screens that included every channel imaginable, complimented by every premium service its premium customers could want.

Below the hotel rooms, on floors three through five, were shops catering to the limousine set. Jewelry, shoes that cost a year's income for most Americans, and haute couture. Lots of haute couture. There was even a Rolls Royce outlet where cars could be ordered with very specific customization and delivered by personal driver anywhere in the world.

The second floor was a club, if it could be called that. So exclusive it had no sign, no bouncer (one does not bounce anyone who makes it to this door), and no sound — the walls inside were soundproofed so completely and efficiently that only when the large oak doors were opened did anyone outside know there was something going on in there.

The first floor, which was the only floor the general public ever got to see, was where Corinne and Lydia headed that day. The restaurant on the Broome Street side was named after its beyond-celebrity chef. Constantine Anastas was Greek by heritage but did not serve Greek food. Instead, the 28-year-old culinary superstar had created what he called Progressive American cuisine. It had a hot new sound to it, and it drew a hot new crowd. The restaurant had opened the same day as the hotel; reservations had been made six months in advance and kept the restaurant impossible to get into. It was now April, and while it could not be said business had died down (to even whisper such a thing was a death knell to a restaurant of this caliber and reputation, and a grave insult to Constantine Anastas), you could get in with no more than a three week wait.

Lydia and Corinne had planned their escapade for over a month. Everything had to fall into place and stay there — no last minute illnesses, no sudden plans by their parents to take them out of school to go somewhere, no unexpected deaths in the family. As April 23rd came closer the girls grew more concerned that something would go wrong. They'd read that Justin Timberlake (admittedly aging out of their demographic but a heartthrob for both of them) was in town shooting a movie and Constantine was his favorite place to have lunch when he wasn't on set. Would he be there? Would Amy Adams, or Jake Gyllenhaal, or even Seth Rogen, sitting at a table with an agent or publicist, while Corinne and Lydia discreetly watched them from across the room? Surely someone — several *someones — would be there the same day they were, since Constantine had more star power in it on a regular afternoon than most top-flight Manhattan eateries saw in a week.*

"Don't be obvious," Corinne said as they crawled out of the cab. Each of them had a backpack as part of the ruse (they couldn't leave home for school looking like they were going to a movie premiere and carrying nothing but red leather clutches).

"My mom's friends with a friend of Julia Roberts," Lydia said dryly. "I know how to act around stars."

Corinne wrinkled her nose. "Julia Roberts was a star, like, forever ago." She gave the cab driver a $20 bill and told him to keep the change, which was significant. They may not be arriving in a motorcade, but they could still act the part.

The entrance to Constantine was deliberately low key. Its diners were accustomed to red carpets and the glare of camera flashes, the sort of gaudy public performance they came here to escape. And while it was true some of them notified the paparazzi they were arriving at a certain time for a certain meal with a certain someone, the true celebrities made quiet entrances and expected an hour or three away from stares and autograph seekers.

Corinne led the way into the restaurant, holding the big glass front door open just long enough for Lydia to take the door handle. Upon entering, they immediately heard chatter and very low music. Chef Constantine had started a new craze among the elite dining crowd: quiet restaurants. For several years the average human eardrum had been under assault in trendy restaurants on both coasts, but people grew tired of having to shout across a small table at the person they were eating with, and Constantine had taken note. It was part of his Progressive American experience.

"Copley, party of two," Corinne said to the maître d', a thin Asian man with a jet black ponytail and eyeglasses Corinne pegged in the $1000 range.

He glanced at his mounted iPad, said, "Of course," and nodded to his underling to seat them. She was as elegant as he was, mid-thirties and looking like she could walk any catwalk in Paris and probably had. The big difference was that she smiled. Constantine was known for drilling niceness into his staff: if people think you consider yourself better than they are, they won't come back. Especially when they're making $15 million for a six week movie shoot.

They followed the woman into the restaurant, which was filled to its hundred seat capacity. Lydia gasped as she glanced at a table near the central fireplace, which had a gas fire going year-round.

"Don't stare," Corinne said. She'd noticed him, too: the lead singer of Third Sun, a boy band of meteoric success when boy bands had been declared dead. He was a very hot, very volatile nineteen-year-old from Canada who looked to be behaving himself today. His group's current song had just broken records on every music download service available.

"I want him," Lydia said, tagging closely behind Corinne as they made their way to a two-top.

"He's gay."

"You don't know that!"

"My uncle Phil's gay and he knows these things," Corinne said, referring to her father's brother who lived in Chicago with his partner Renaldo.

The elegant ex-model stopped at a beautifully appointed table and eased a chair out for Corinne.

"Thank you," Corinne said.

"My name's Sasha," the woman said, smiling again. "Your server will be Steven, and if you need anything at all he'll provide that for you ladies. I'm at your service as well, of course. Please enjoy."

Lydia frowned slightly when her own chair had not been pulled out for her. "What am I, chopped liver?" she said.

"She's nice," Corinne replied. "They're all very nice, don't take it personally."

No sooner had Lydia taken her seat than Steven glided up silently with two menus. "For you," he said, handing a leather-bound menu to Corinne, "and one for you, Madam. May I get you something to drink first? A soda, perhaps?"

He clearly knew the girls were nowhere near drinking age. Lydia was disappointed; she'd thought of ordering a Cosmo for the *occasion. She'd never had one, but her mother liked them and always looked like she was having a good time with one in front of her.*

"Sparkling water's fine for us," Corinne said, cutting off any discussion of what to drink.

"Right away," Steven said, then he turned and glided back into the crowd.

"I'm hungry," Lydia said. She opened the menu, glanced quickly over it. "Why aren't there any prices?"

Corinne stared at her. "You're joking, right?"

Lydia was not joking. She'd been saving for a month to pay for this lunch and was suddenly worried it would not be enough.

"I'll pick up the difference," Corinne said, reading Lydia's expression. "My uncle Phil who knows the lead singer for Third Sun is gay sent me two hundred dollars for my birthday."

Lydia relaxed and took another look at the menu, trying to decide which Progressive American specialty she was going to have today.

CHAPTER Fifteen

It had been well over three years since the Oasis Hotel and its centerpiece restaurant Constantine had opened to press releases, digital flashbulbs and furious buzz. It didn't look any older—the hotel had been built from the ground up just for this purpose. Three years may be rough on Manhattan architecture but it was not long enough to age an infant building. The tall glass windows lining the hotel were still spotless. The awning looked like it was replaced with a new one every few months. A red carpet, installed and kept for pretense, still protected very expensive shoes from the pavement as they click-clicked their way into the lobby. And the doormen still wore white gloves, their burgundy suits spotless and their smiles fixed.

Kyle and Linda arrived just before one-thirty. There had been a delay with the subway, a sick passenger on a train ahead of them. Kyle thought this was just as well, since the lunch crowd might be thinning now, at least from diners who had jobs to get back to.

They entered the restaurant. Having never been there, they didn't know nothing had changed since the day Corinne Copley and Lydia Becker ate lunch there. The same tables, the same table settings, even the same faux tulip centerpieces. But extremely well crafted faux tulips: only a botanist could tell they weren't real.

A pleasant, crisply dressed and professionally smooth maître d' welcomed them. He did not look like the Samuel Wong identified in the police reports: he wasn't Asian.

"Name please?" he asked, gliding his finger over an iPad at the front podium.

"We don't have a reservation," Linda said.

"We're not here to eat, actually," Kyle added.

"The hotel entrance is on West Broadway," the man said.

"We're not here for that, either," Kyle said. "We're hoping to just ask a few questions."

The man looked at them. "Of me?"

"Well, no," Kyle said. "Does Samuel Wong still work here?"

The man grimaced, his nose curling as if he'd just smelled something unpleasant.

"Sam hasn't worked here for two years. They need the best, and that's me. My name's Edwin, by the way."

Linda glanced into the dining room behind Edwin. Half the tables were empty; she wondered what they needed the best for.

"Okay," Kyle said. "So Sam's gone. Is there anyone who was working here three years ago?" He could tell by Edwin's reaction that he was wondering why they needed to speak to someone. "I'm Kyle Callahan, a reporter, and this is my friend, Linda Sikorsky."

"A private investigator," Linda said, adding to the ruse.

"It's about a cold case we're looking into. The death of a young woman who ate here the day she was killed."

Edwin's eyes widened. He knew about that story, everybody did.

"Sasha was here then," he said. "Let me get her for you."

He left them and hurried toward the back of the restaurant.

"Fancy schmancy," Linda said, looking around. "But half empty. What's the big deal?"

"Whatever it was, it's not such a big deal anymore," Kyle replied. "Stars rise and stars fall."

A moment later Edwin returned, followed closely by a beautiful woman in a cream pantsuit.

"This is Sasha," Edwin said. Then, to Sasha, "This is Mr. Callahan, he's with the news, and this is Linda—I didn't quite catch your last name—she's a private detective. They wanted to ask you some questions about that misfortunate girl who was murdered three years ago."

Kyle saw a moment of fear flash in Sasha's eyes. Wherever she had immigrated from, Kyle guessed it was not a place where talking to reporters was a good idea, and she had certainly talked to a few in relation to Corinne's murder.

"I don't know anything," Sasha said. "I told the nice officers that, more than once."

"Would you mind telling us then, one more time? It won't take long."

"Please," Edwin interjected, "have a seat at the bar, it's quiet."

That's an understatement, Linda thought, looking at the long bar that lined one wall. It had a dozen tall, elegant stools and no one sitting on them.

Sasha hesitated, then led Kyle and Linda to the bar. "Please give us some privacy," she said to the bartender. He quietly moved to the far end, out of earshot.

For the next ten minutes Sasha repeated what she'd told the police. There wasn't much to tell: she was on duty that day, she remembered Corinne and Lydia. She seated them, then turned their service over to Steven, who had also since left the restaurant. She'd only noticed them again when they were about to leave.

"What was it that made you notice them then?" Kyle asked.

"The one girl, not the dead one—is that the way to say that?—she was unhappy. I think she didn't like it here. And there was something about the check. I saw her counting out cash on the table and looking worried, like she didn't have enough money. Then the other girl …"

"The dead one," Linda offered.

"Yes," said Sasha, "that one. Very pretty, by the way, such a shame what happened to her. She paid the bill and they left. And that's it, that's all I know."

It had been as unhelpful as visiting the bakery. Linda knew from experience that retracing someone's footsteps could be as uneventful as it had been for the person you were following. Until, of course, the robbery and murder. She had begun to doubt they would find anything the police and reporters had not found. The death of Corinne Copley was shaping up to remain unsolved and as cold as her father's heart had become. She didn't want to say this to Kyle, not yet, but by the end of the day she would tell him it was probably time to let go.

"Thank you for talking to us," Kyle said. He slid off the stool.

"No problem," Sasha replied. She was relieved to have gotten this over quickly. She did not like reliving events she had nothing to do with besides witnessing, and she had witnessed nothing of significance.

"Excuse me," she said. "I need to return to my job."

Sasha headed toward a far corner of the restaurant. Apparently her job included walking around the half-empty restaurant looking as if she was at every diner's beck and call.

"Let's go," Kyle said, leading Linda toward the front exit. Edwin was at the podium, looking as busy as one can look with nothing to do.

"Thank you," Linda said to the maître d.

"My pleasure," said Edwin, barely glancing up from his iPad screen.

They walked out onto Broome Street. Kyle felt and looked dejected. Had they just wasted three hours of their day covering old ground? Were they headed down a dead end?

"Where to now?" Linda asked. The sooner they found themselves on 37th Street where Corinne had been killed, the sooner she could gently tell Kyle this case would not be solved, not by them.

"I'm thinking," Kyle said. He stood in front of the restaurant. He looked east, then west, letting his mind wander ever so slightly. "This way," he finally said, heading back toward West Broadway.

"Where are we going?" asked Linda.

"To the subway. But I'm looking for something first."

This made Linda curious. They'd learned nothing at the bakery and even less at the restaurant. "What are you looking for, Kyle?"

He thought a moment, then said, "A famous apartment building."

Linda remembered Lydia telling them the girls had stopped in front of a building to take pictures. But Manhattan was filled with buildings, many of them famous. And how long could it have taken to stop for photographs? What could there possibly be in it that had anything to do with what happened?

"You're sure you want to spend time on this?" Linda said.

"No," replied Kyle, "I'm not. But it's *not* spending time on it that worries me. They all missed something, Linda. Somewhere along the way they all missed something, and I'm not going to."

He was right and she knew it. The Devil is in the details, and the murderer — or at least the motive — is in the police reports. Buried somewhere in scribbles and the recollections of witnesses. It had been her experience for her entire professional life. If they were going to do this, no matter the outcome, they could not afford to overlook what everyone else had.

They walked slowly toward the subway several blocks away. Somewhere between the restaurant and the steps leading down to the train there was a famous apartment building. Kyle wished he'd paid more attention to these things. He knew the Dakota — that's where John Lennon was assassinated. Plenty of costly high-rises with the name Trump plastered on them. But what well-known apartment building was in this neighborhood?

Then he saw it. The Centurion. Not tall, not massive, but very, very famous.

"Come," Kyle said to Linda, picking up his pace. "I think I know where they took those pictures."

Linda had to hurry to keep up. She saw the building a half block up, an American flag fluttering on a tall pole in front.

And she saw the guard house: the building's entrance was set back, at the center of a circular driveway protected by gates on each side and a small, single guard station.

They'd found what Kyle was looking for.

CHAPTER Sixteen

"That's it?" Lydia said as they paid their check. Other than the cute lead singer for Third Sun they had not seen one major celebrity on the outing they'd planned and invested in for so long. And he was no longer of interest to Lydia. She didn't have any problem with his gayness, but it pretty much took him off her fantasy list.

"I think I saw the anchor for Channel 4 walk by," Corinne said. She, too, had been less than impressed and was trying to put a positive spin on it.

"What's his name if he's so famous?"

"Her."

"Fine," harrumphed Lydia. "Her name."

"I don't know off the top of my head. She auditioned to join The Chat, I know that."

The Chat was a new morning program with four women in a living room set, several years after women's talk shows were passé.

"Great, I'll be sure to record it."

Lydia was in an increasingly sour mood. The food had been amazing and the check eye-popping. Corinne had picked up the difference, as she'd promised. Lydia's $50, all she had left after their morning at the bakery and some light shopping, did not cover her half. Lydia had ordered the most expensive steak burger in New York City, made with American Kobe beef, complimented with high mountain potato fries, whatever they were, and a $25 Mesa Verde salad, whatever that was. Corinne had enjoyed the same salad and fresh water shark tacos, unconvinced that there was such a thing as a fresh water shark.

"Do you get the feeling they just make this stuff up and charge crazy prices for it?" Lydia said, watching Corinne count out $135 in cash for the check, tip included.

"Probably. But wasn't it amazing?"

Lydia shrugged. She would have been more satisfied with a chili dog and fries from the Shake Hut. She felt ripped off, mostly by the absence of anyone she might read about online the next day. It seemed the celebrities had come early, seen, conquered, and ridden away in their limousines a few months ago. Rich tourists and suckers like herself and Corinne were the only ones coming here now – though they came in large numbers. She suspected they'd catch on soon enough and Constantine Anastas would have to adjust his menu or his prices to stay in business.

They paid the check and waded through the tables, quite a few of them now empty as the lunch hour ended. Corinne noticed how many of the diners were in upscale office attire, and she realized the stars they'd hoped to see, descended from the heights for a quick Mesa Verde salad and a dolphin quesadilla, had been replaced by the well-heeled but pedestrian professional class. Lawyers, corporate vice presidents, and more lawyers. This was not what she and Lydia had in mind when they began planning the outing – a clandestine outing at that. Nobody knew they were there. They'd sworn each other to silence: no Instagram photos, no texts to friends. Now, of course, it was for the best. What was she supposed to tweet? That she'd just had lunch sitting next to a bankruptcy attorney? How unexciting was that!

They exited onto Broome Street and stood together outside the restaurant. The hotel entrance was at the corner and they could see guests arriving, welcomed by bellmen in dark suits with thin white stripes running the length of their coats and pants. White gloves, helping "Madame" and "Sir" from black sedans, hailing taxis to take tourists from Indiana, who'd no doubt scrimped and saved for a year to spend one week at the Oasis, off to the Empire State building or a Wednesday matinee of The Lion King.

"Kinda sucks, doesn't it?" Lydia said.

"Kinda."

Corinne looked at her watch: 2:30 p.m. She was having dinner at Maria's Cantina at 7:00 with Gilda. Six friends were celebrating Gilda's birthday. Lydia was not invited and didn't know about it – another secret. Corinne suddenly felt guilty for the secrets and … omissions. For surely they weren't lies, she told herself. She hadn't lied to her parents about coming to Constantine. Right? She hadn't said she was going to school. She just hadn't said she was not going to school. And she hadn't told Lydia she wasn't invited to Gilda's birthday dinner. She just hadn't told her anything.

This put Corinne in a bind. She had four hours to kill and hadn't thought about what she was going to do with them. She did not want to go home. Skipping school was something she never did and she wanted to make the most of it. She'd assumed Lydia would stay with her, then realized that by not asking for Lydia to be invited to dinner it put them on divergent paths. She couldn't very well hang out with Lydia for four more hours and then abruptly abandon her for a party she wasn't invited to.

"Where now?" Corinne said, hoping Lydia would suggest they go window shopping on Fifth Avenue or a stroll along the Chelsea Piers.

"Home," Lydia said, still in a funk from the disappointing lunch.

This surprised Corinne. "You can't go home, school's not out for another hour."

"There's nobody at home, remember?"

This was true, and for a moment Corinne considered heading home herself. But she'd broken the rules; she'd gone to a not-so-fabulous restaurant in an obscenely expensive hotel and nobody knew about it. She felt guilty. Home would just remind her it was all pretty much for nothing. She was out eighty-five dollars just for lunch, she'd not seen anyone worth naming, and she had four hours before dinner.

"I'll walk you to the subway," Corinne said. There wasn't much else to do about it, and she knew Lydia would not change her mind. Her second-best friend felt betrayed by circumstances, and if she knew where Corinne was headed that night she'd feel truly betrayed. It made Corinne a bit queasy. She was a nice person, a good girl. After all, she hadn't told Lydia about Gilda's dinner because Gilda didn't like Lydia! Corinne was sparing her the pain of exclusion.

"Fine," Lydia said, "let's go. I've never seen so many nobodies with so much money, it's disgusting."

The girls headed up West Broadway toward the subway that would take Lydia uptown. Corinne had decided to walk wherever she was going. She had plenty of time and no plans.

"You didn't take any pictures," Lydia said.

"Neither did you," said Corinne.

"Of what? A stockbroker having tuna tartar with his mistress? I don't think so."

It was true. Neither of them had taken any photos with their XG4 phones, the best and newest on the market, which both of them had. Corinne had planned to snap at least a dozen, but waited until they were seated. She wanted to get a picture of Taylor or Brad or Kanye, but none of them showed. So she found herself at the end of a huge letdown with nothing to show for it — literally — and not upset about it. Lydia was right. Stockbrokers with their secret girlfriends (and in at least one case a boyfriend, from what Corinne deduced), were not the stuff of Facebook. Who wants their friends to ask who that stranger was at the next table?

"We have to get at least one picture," Corinne said, digging her phone out of her purse.

"One, for posterity," said Lydia. "And nobody ever sees it."

"Fine."

They were strolling past one of the most famous apartment buildings in Manhattan. The Centurion had been built in the early 1900s and was home to some of the most celebrated, wealthy and powerful people in New York City. At only six stories, it was also very exclusive: space was limited and came at a premium-of-premiums. The front of the building had a short, circular driveway for privacy, and a small guard station, manned 24/7 by men who looked more suited to combat than to building security. The architecture spoke of a time when architecture was grand, overstated and set in stone — limestone, marble, exotic rock. A series of gargoyles looked down on the street, as intimidating as the man in the guard booth.

They stopped on the sidewalk in front of the building.

"Let's get a picture with the guard," Corinne said. She waved at the man and was rewarded with a suspicious scowl.

"He looks like he'd shoot us," Lydia said. "The sidewalk's fine."

Having settled the issue, Corinne pulled Lydia close to her. She took her phone, reversed the camera, and adjusted their image in the screen.

"Smile," Corinne said.

"I haven't smiled since we got to the restaurant," Lydia replied, quickly fussing with her hair when she saw their image.

"Then it'll be good for you."

The girls smiled; Corinne snapped the photo. "One more," she said, and took another.

With that they continued up the street.

The guard noticed them but made nothing of it. Tourists were always taking pictures outside the building. No one ever asked him about the two teenage girls taking photos outside the Centurion that day. No one but the guard even knew they took them.

Almost no one.

CHAPTER Seventeen

The Centurion wasn't the oldest of the celebrity apartment buildings in Manhattan, those buildings whose names were as well-known as the tenants who'd lived in them over the decades, nor was it by any means the largest. There was the Dakota, The Eldorado and the massive London Terrace, but the Centurion held its own and attracted its share of tourists wanting a photograph of the building where Mick Jagger spent a summer of elegant debauchery and where Melinda Lockland, once the biggest name in country music, was found dead in a tenant's bathtub with a syringe in her arm. It had long been among the popular stops on walking tours of Tribeca and SoHo, and remained protected by round-the-clock guards in its small front guard station. The circular driveway had seen more limousines than could be counted, and absolutely no one got inside who didn't live there or arrived in a private ambulance.

Kyle and Linda stood on the sidewalk for several minutes, looking up at the building. It stood only six stories tall, a minor star in the constellation of Manhattan architectural wonders, but it burned brightly and boasted a guest list second to few.

"They don't make buildings like this anymore," Kyle said, staring at the gargoyles that watched over the building. It was cliché but true. Architects and builders had eschewed such detail since at least the 1950s. The 60s saw the introduction of boredom and blandness, incarceration-chic for public housing, glass for anything remotely corporate — tall, flat, unimaginative glass in sheets by the thousand. The Centurion was both a throwback and a marvel.

"Who lives here?" Linda asked, watching a small group of tourists being led by a guide. They stopped across the street and the guide pointed at the building, telling them its history in a voice too far off for Linda to make out what he was saying.

"I don't know," said Kyle. "Lots of famous people have, and I'm sure they still do. It's why the girls wanted a picture that day — or at least Corinne did. Follow me …"

Kyle headed for the guard booth. The guard was a short, muscular man in a brown uniform, hat and brass name tag pinned to his lapel identifying him as Henry. Aging, but doing it well. He had a moustache, and he watched them approach with a mixture of indifference and professionalism: he'd turned away hundreds of curiosity seekers in his fifteen years in the guard booth. He was expecting to do it once again with the man and woman walking toward him. Politely but firmly.

"May I help you?" he said. He took their measure with a quick glance, and Kyle had the sense he was scanning for weapons.

"I was wondering …" Kyle said.

"Everyone's wondering," Henry replied. "That's why they stop here. Do you have an appointment with one of the our tenants?"

"No," Linda said. "We just had some questions."

He can't very well say he's busy right now, Linda thought. *He stands in a box all day.*

"I'm not really here to answer questions," said Henry.

"We understand that," Kyle said. "But it's not about the building or anyone who lives here. It's about two young girls who took some photographs here a while back."

Henry was unimpressed. He had witnessed thousands of people taking photographs in front of the building. "You're serious?" he said.

"Oh, they're not just any girls," Linda offered. "One of them was murdered later that day."

Henry, while he would never admit it, was a bored man, at least for most of the hours he spent in his guard booth. A murder, or questions about one, would probably be the most interesting thing he experienced all day.

"Which girls were these, and why would I remember them?"

Kyle said, "The shooting death of one of them made national news."

Recognition flickered in Henry's eyes. "You mean the young woman who was killed for her cell phone."

Of course he knew; everyone knew who read a newspaper, watched a television news report or scanned — as most now did — online news websites.

"Yes," Kyle said. "Her name was Corinne Copley."

"Are you a reporter? Or a policeman?"

"Both, actually," Linda said. "I'm Linda Sikorsky, retired homicide detective, and this is Kyle Callahan, he's with a TV station here in the city." She extended her hand. "We're looking into this as a cold case and were told the girls stopped here that afternoon. Or, at least, in front of this building, for some pictures."

Henry shook both their hands, then said, "It's about time."

"Excuse me?" said Kyle.

"I've been waiting ever since that happened for someone to come around asking questions, but no one ever did."

"Really?" asked Linda.

"Really. I assumed they didn't think it was important. Hell, I didn't think it was important. That's why I never went to the police. So many people stop here and take pictures that I thought, well, they were just two more — the girls, I mean."

"You thought it wasn't important so you never told anyone," Kyle said.

"Yes and no. I told lots of people! My wife, my brother. They said, 'Henry, you ought to go to the police,' but I was, like, with what? What is there to tell, except that poor girl who got shot stopped in front of the Centurion for two minutes. Less, probably, maybe a minute."

Kyle thought about it a moment. "So they didn't encounter anyone? You didn't notice anyone who looked like he was following them?"

"No," Henry said. "It was a quiet day. Weekdays usually are, and the kids were in school. Most of them, anyway — obviously these two weren't, but that's none of my business. They stopped for a minute, took some, what do you call them now, 'selfies'? And they walked on."

It was probably nothing, Kyle thought. Just a stop along the deadly path Corinne took that day. On the other hand, no one else had discovered this — not the police, not the reporters, not even Skate, who had been obsessed with his daughter's death for three years. Was there something about this stop, that moment in time, that was connected to what happened?

"Who lives here?" Kyle said, looking past Henry to the main entrance of the Centurion.

Henry frowned. "I'm not at liberty to say."

"You can tell us," Linda said. "We're not tourists, we won't tell anyone."

"I take my job very seriously," Henry said, frowning. "I have been on duty here for fifteen years, and I plan on staying until my retirement. I certainly won't risk that to tell you what I have told no one else in all this time. Divulging information about the tenants, including their names, is strictly forbidden."

Kyle sighed. They could surely find out who lived in the building if they put a little effort into searching, but that would have to wait. It also would probably not reveal anything but a short list of high profile tenants, none of whom had any connection to Corinne Copley.

"Thank you for your time," Kyle said.

"Certainly," Henry replied.

Kyle touched Linda on the arm and headed back to the street.

"That's it?" Linda said, as they started walking uptown.

"There's nothing more to learn there," Kyle said. "For now. And probably not later. They took some photos, they moved on, and that's what we need to do."

"Where are we moving on to?" Linda asked, quickening her pace to keep up with him.

"The cupcake shop, and the movie theater."

Kyle knew from the notes and reports that once Lydia left for home Corinne continued on, stopping at a place called Cathy's Cup and Cake in Chelsea, then to Chelsea Cinemas for a movie to pass the time. *If only she'd gone home,* Kyle thought. But that was life, the very essence of coincidence that lies at the heart of human existence. If only we had been somewhere we weren't, if only we had *not* been there, if only we had gone left instead of right. He thought back to meeting Danny that first time at the Katherine Pride Gallery. If he had not been there, if Danny had not come around a corner and bumped into him, spilling both their drinks, sputtering an apology as they looked at each other, they would not be married now. That was how their life together began. *If only.*

Kyle kept walking, hoping the fresh air would clear the clutter in his mind. He needed space there, just enough for the unexpected thought, the sudden insight. He hoped it would come; he needed it to come. And when it did, this sad, cold case might finally begin to warm.

CHAPTER Eighteen

Corinne was not happy about being abandoned by Lydia and considered bumping her to third or even fourth best friend. She also knew her anger wouldn't last. She couldn't really expect Lydia to stay with her all day, and there was that sticky situation with the dinner party. It was more the way Lydia just left her there, pecking her on the cheek and rushing down into the subway to catch the train they heard pulling into the station. Bye, Lydia! Bye, fun day that wasn't! Bye, allowance she'd saved weeks to spend at a restaurant she would be saying not-nice things about on Yelp tomorrow. Not mean things, necessarily, but c'mon. No big names, no hot guys eating alone, not much of anything but very good food at very high prices.

She didn't want to travel far alone. She considered going to the Met by herself, but quickly decided walking around the museum with no one to talk to was lame. She liked looking at art well enough, but she'd been there a million times and thought it was better suited for visits from out-of-town relatives and family friends. Her parents had plenty of those. After walking uptown several blocks, she remembered there was a new movie out she wanted to see. It was playing in Chelsea, she knew that, and Chelsea wasn't far from Hell's Kitchen, where she was having dinner. If she walked slowly she'd get to the three-thirty show, watch the movie (going light on the popcorn) and get out just in time to head to Maria's Cantina. That was a good plan.

She didn't start feeling followed until she was almost at the movie theater. She stopped at Cathy's Cup and Cake just to look at the cupcakes — they were famous and had made the top of NYC Magazine's Best of the Best list. She wasn't about to eat one. She was still full from lunch and knew she'd be unable to watch a movie without at least a small popcorn and a flavored water. But looking was fine.

She was standing back from the small line of customers, peering between them into the glass bakery case, when she first had the sense *of someone looking at her from outside the shop. Watching her. She glanced up at the man and he quickly turned away, walking out of sight past the store window. Had he been watching her? And why would she think that, anyway? Men watched women all the time. They watched girls. Some of them watched children, for godsake. Corinne knew she was good-looking. She'd had her share of stares and more than a few catcalls. But there was just something extra creepy about this guy.*

You're imagining things, Corinne, stop it, she told herself. He was probably looking at the same things you were, those luscious cupcakes and pastries, just from a different angle. Maybe he's broke. Maybe he's homeless and hungry and you should be ashamed of yourself for judging him. Or maybe he's waiting for someone. You'll go outside and he'll be there talking to his girlfriend. Or his boyfriend, more likely. She chuckled. This was Chelsea, after all.

"May I help you?" a man's voice said.

Corinne looked up, startled to be spoken to. She realized the bakery was almost empty, just one woman left paying for her purchase. The voice belonged to one of three people working there – two women and the man asking her if she wanted anything.

"No, thanks," Corinne replied. "I'd love to but I've got a dinner to go to. Next time for sure."

"We'll be here."

"Hey," she said, "Can I ask you something?"

"Go right ahead," the man said.

"Did you see someone outside just now, I don't know ... staring at me?"

He cocked his head; it was an odd question. People stared at other people all the time – there were about eight million sets of eyes in New York City, they had to look somewhere.

"No, sorry," he said. "I'm kinda busy, I didn't notice anyone outside."

She felt stupid having asked, and having worried about it in the first place, so she waved goodbye to the cashier and quickly walked outside.

She'd been right. The man, while not a figment of her imagination, was not waiting for her. She stood outside the bakery on 7th Avenue and looked to her left, then to her right. Lots of people, but no thin, twitchy, ghostly looking man waiting for her.

She shook her head, telling herself to get a grip. She thought about taking her phone out of her purse and texting Lydia to see if she was home yet. She thought, too, about texting her father, but … damnit. This is what happens when you break the rules. This is what happens when you cut class and spend a day on the lamb.

You're not on the lamb, idiot, she said to herself, hoping it hadn't been out loud. People on the lamb are running from someone. You're not running from anyone. You're just having a fun day to yourself. Make the most of it.

She headed uptown. Two more blocks and she'd turn left on 23rd Street, another long block and she'd be at the movie. Caroline's Say wasn't high on her list of movies to see, but it had gotten positive reviews and she could use a good comedy. Or at least a few laughs. The movie was about a twenty-something woman trying to make it as an actress in Los Angeles and all the ups and downs of her life, in which, of course, she had her say. Clever. Walking toward the theater she decided she would tell her parents that night after dinner what she'd done. It wasn't like her, and she knew they'd only be angry for about a half day, but the sooner she came clean, the sooner she could post her photos and tweet and text and share her law-breaking ways with her friends. She smiled at the thought of being an outlaw, just as she made it to 23rd Street and went west.

He watched her turn the corner, hanging back enough to disappear into a doorway if she turned around. She'd seen him outside the bakery and that was not good. He considered himself a professional, no matter what anyone else thought of him, which was not much. He did what he was told, and he did it well. He stayed alive, too; that was his first mission in life: not dying. Death came in a dozen ways for people like him, some of them expected, many of them not. Avoiding an untimely demise had not been easy. Not nearly as easy as this was going to be. What was it his sorry excuse for a mother always told him? Patience is a virtue. Yeah, well, she was dead. She could afford to be patient now. And he could afford to wait just a little while longer. Wait till the girl was in the right place at the right time. Wait till dark if he had to. He would just keep *following her and hope she wasn't heading home, wherever that was. He'd have to make his move before then or suffer the consequences.*

He was most relieved to see her walk to the movie theater ticket box. This was good. This gave him time to think and plan. Time to practice his patience.

CHAPTER Nineteen

Cathy's Cup and Cake was on a stretch of Seventh Avenue in Chelsea, a neighborhood Kyle had seen change dramatically over the past twenty years. Once an industrial neighborhood filled with blue collar workers, Chelsea had fallen on hard times in the 1970s, along with the rest of the city. Then, slowly, it became the alternative to Greenwich Village as the rents there steadily escalated into the stratosphere. Gay people and bohemians began filtering uptown, north of 14th Street, and over the course of a decade Chelsea became Manhattan's biggest gay neighborhood. As with anywhere this happened, once the gays settled the neighborhood it began to gentrify. Other people moved in, people with baby strollers, men and women who worked in the financial industry, then at its height of influence and domination of the city's economy. Finally, after two decades of this, Chelsea was one of the most expensive places in the city to live, and the poor gays, the poor bohemians, the people with baby strollers handed down from their relatives, moved further north, planting their rainbow flags in Hell's Kitchen and taking apartments in Washington Heights, Inwood, and finally out of Manhattan altogether.

Kyle and Linda arrived at the cupcake shop mid-afternoon, when there wasn't much business. Unlike Eighth Avenue just one long block west, Seventh Avenue never had that much foot traffic. Eighth was the pulsing heart of Chelsea (complete with clogged arteries and the signs of age and stress); Seventh was its second cousin, its spare bedroom. Cathy's Cup and Cake had managed to stay in business for five years, an impressive feat anywhere in the city, but especially here. Most of the stores and restaurants surrounding it had come and gone several times, under a long list of names. Tucked between a corner bodega and one of the city's ubiquitous nail salons, Cathy's offered cupcakes, coffee and comfort. That's why people still went there, despite the cupcake craze being descendant among the smart-watch and kale salad crowd. Some customers didn't care if a day's calorie allotment came in one delicious, butter-frosted cupcake, and others treated it as a guilty pleasure.

An old fashioned bell rang when they entered, affixed to the top of the door like the bell around a cat's neck. Only two customers were there, eating at one of three small tables on offer. One tall, lanky man was behind the counter going over invoices. A woman who looked like his twin was loading fresh cupcakes into the large glass display case. Kyle could smell the bakery in back: these were cupcakes delivered straight from the oven to the customers' mouths. At least two men were in back stirring and baking and cleaning up for the next round.

"Afternoon," the man said. He looked to be in his forties, with graying hair tied back in a ponytail. "Just got some new ones out. You won't find any better."

"I know," Kyle said, walking up to the counter. "You were voted Best Cupcakes in New York City."

"Two years in a row," the man said. "We're on all the cupcake tours, too. But those are dwindling."

Kyle liked the fact he was very chatty.

"I'm Kyle," he said. "Kyle Callahan. And this is my friend, Linda Sikorsky."

Linda nodded.

The man offered his hand to them both. "Dave," he said.

"Is there a Cathy?" Linda asked, referring to the shop's name.

"That would be my mother," Dave said. "This started with her recipes."

"I'm sure she's happy about that," said Kyle.

"She would be. She passed away six years ago. This was my way of carrying on, making sure a small part of the world knew who she was."

"Very nice," said Linda. It made her think of her own store named after her father. It was a way of keeping their memories alive. She liked this man.

"So what'll you have?" asked Dave.

"Actually," said Kyle, "we were hoping to ask a few questions."

Dave smiled. "Nobody gets the recipe. And believe me, they've tried."

"It's not about the cupcakes. It's about a young woman who came in here three years ago."

"Hmm. We get young women in here all the time. Old women, too. Men, kids."

"This one was unique," Linda said. "Her name was Corinne Copley."

Dave looked at them, thinking. "I know that name. Wasn't she the girl who got killed? For her phone or something?"

"That's her," said Kyle. "She stopped in here that day, and I thought maybe she spoke to you, or maybe you noticed something unusual. If you were even here …"

"I'm always here," Dave said. "Five in the morning till ten at night. And yes, I remember her. Who could forget, once it was on the news? She seemed perfectly fine to me. But she did ask me a strange question."

Kyle and Linda waited.

"She asked me if I saw a man staring at her from outside."

Eureka, thought Kyle. "And did you? See someone?"

"No," Dave said. "I looked out, and, you know, we're very busy in here, depending on the time of day. We had five, six people in the store when she came in. I looked out when she asked me, but there was no one there. I figured she was imagining it, until I saw them talking about her … on the news, you know."

Kyle was thinking it through. Somewhere between lunch at Constantine and stopping here for a cupcake, if she bought one, Corinne Copley picked up a stalker. Or a follower. A man, staring at her. Maybe this was the first place he saw her.

That happens—disturbed men, predators, see a vulnerable woman, or a child, and they become immediately fixated, sometimes dangerously so. In this case it proved fatal. If, that is, he'd actually been there, and if he's the same man who followed her to 37th Street.

"I wish I could be more helpful," Dave said. "I told the cops, that Detective Dietz. I assumed they followed up on it, but no one was ever arrested."

Kyle, too, assumed they followed up on it and wondered where the trail went cold; or, more likely, there had been no trail to begin with. Corinne noticed a man starting at her, and then what? The man was never seen again. Or the man had been deep in thought while his gaze was fixed on her—that happens a lot, too. People sometimes think they're being stared at when in reality they just happen to be in the line of sight of someone lost in a daydream.

Or he was following her.

"Thank you very much," Kyle said.

"I didn't give you anything to thank me for," Dave said. "At least have a cupcake."

Dave got a small box and put two large cupcakes in it.

"Make it three," Kyle said, thinking of Danny. "I'll pay you, of course."

"No, you won't," said Dave, tying the box with string and handing it to Linda. "I've been a little haunted ever since that happened, wishing I'd seen a man outside, wishing I'd been able to give the police a description. 'Cause, you know, once she was killed, I knew … I just *knew* … she hadn't imagined it."

Kyle knew it, too. The man outside the cupcake shop had been real. He had followed Corinne, and he had killed her.

Kyle thanked Dave a last time and led Linda out onto the street. He stood on Seventh Avenue, looking south, then north.

"You think he was real," Linda said.

"I do," said Kyle. "Maybe this is where he saw her using her phone. It was the phone he wanted, remember."

"True. But she didn't use her phone that day, Lydia told us that."

"She did use it," Kyle corrected her. "Twice."

Linda knew he was right.

"Once to take pictures," she said, "and once when she was killed for it. You think there's a connection?"

"There has to be. Or maybe he just wanted the phone. It didn't have a kill switch then, none of them did."

"A kill switch?" Linda had read about those.

"Yes. It gives a phone's owner the ability to …"

"I know what it is," Linda said. "And I know it's happened before. People get mugged for their phones. Sometimes they get killed."

"This time they did," Kyle said, and he began walking toward 23rd Street.

"Where are we going now?" Linda asked.

"One more stop, then I want to go back to where it happened. I want to stand there again."

"And do what?"

"*Listen*," said Kyle. "I just want to stand there and *listen*."

Linda had no idea what he was talking about but she knew he was onto something and needed to think. She followed along silently as they made their way to Chelsea Cinema.

CHAPTER Twenty

Kyle had seen many movies at the theater located near the corner of 23rd Street and Eighth Avenue, all but a few of them forgotten. The name of the chain had changed several times as the multiplex survived through the years. It had been a Regency, then a Clairmont, then a Starland Cinema. If you didn't pay attention you wouldn't notice the name above the front entrance. What was it now? A MetroMax. They were new on the scene and had gobbled up dozens of movie houses across the five boroughs. Whoever owned them was as anonymous as the last owner, and the owner before that, some corporate behemoth headquartered in Seattle or Indianapolis. The only thing that mattered to moviegoers was that it was still in business and the prices had gone up again—slowly, steadily, until a trip to the movies, complete with popcorn and sodas, was nearly as expensive as an Off-Broadway show.

Linda was still holding the box of cupcakes when Kyle went to the window and bought two tickets for a movie. He had no intention of watching it; he wanted to go inside and see if there was anyone old enough to have been here three years ago. Turnover was high, but there were a few older workers who worked at movie theaters to supplement a fixed income or just to pass the time. One man in particular came to mind, an elderly gentleman who had been taking tickets as long as Kyle had lived in New York. Maybe he'd retired early and this was his way of staying busy, or maybe this was the job he'd had all his adult life and he'd reached a sort of platinum status with the various owners.

They walked into the theater and looked around. It was nearly empty on a Thursday afternoon. Only two people staffed the downstairs concession stand; both looked too young to have been out of high school when Corinne was killed.

Then Kyle looked over and saw him, the old man standing at the same station he'd manned for at least two decades. You had to get past him to see any of the movies, and Kyle guessed that no one ever managed to slip by without a ticket. He may be old, Kyle thought, but he notices everything. It's his job.

"Excuse me," Kyle said, walking up to the man.

He was tall, with excellent posture that spoke of professionalism and not a small amount of pride.

"Yes?" the man said, looking at the tickets in Kyle's hand.

Kyle handed him the tickets.

"Theater seven, second floor," the man said.

"Actually," said Kyle, stepping to the side. "We were hoping to ask you a couple questions. I'm Kyle, and this is Linda."

"Pleased to meet you," the man said. He did not offer his name.

"Do you remember the girl who was killed three years ago? The one who was all over the news?"

The man's eyes widened. What was this? Of course he remembered the girl, everybody who paid the least attention to the news remembered her. He'd already answered questions about her, several times, in fact.

"Are you with the police?" he asked.

"No," said Kyle. "Well, Linda used to be, and I'm just a friend of the girl's father."

"I see." The man looked past them, hoping more people would come into the theater so he could tell them he was too busy to talk, but no one came or went.

"She came here to see a movie, we know that," Linda said.

"Yes, she did," the man replied. "I took her ticket. I don't remember what she was here to see. I don't pay much attention to what's showing, or who comes to see it. Movies these days are too vulgar and childish for me. I just remember her because, well …"

"Yes," said Linda gently. "It was terrible."

"Terrible," he said. "What was it you want to ask me that I haven't already answered?"

"Did you see someone follow her in?" Kyle asked.

"I did indeed," he said, surprising them. "And I already said that, to the police, and to a couple of reporters. A skinny guy, came in right after her and left when she did. But I can't say he was following her."

"So why did you notice him?" Kyle asked.

The man shrugged. "I don't know, really. Instinct. I've been doing this job a very long time. I watch people, it's what I do. What they pay me to do. I don't just take tickets. I watch for theft, for people trying to sneak in here, it happens all the time. Kids especially but sometimes the seniors — they think I'll look the other way because they're old like me. Well, I don't."

"So you noticed him," Kyle prodded.

"I did. There was just something about him. About the way he hurried after her. But they never caught anybody, least not as I know."

"You're correct, they did not."

"And you think you're going to."

"I can't say that. I'm just trying to follow in her footsteps."

"Aren't you afraid?" he asked.

"Afraid of what?" said Linda.

"Afraid he'll kill you, too."

Kyle hadn't thought about that. He wasn't sure what he expected. Did he expect to find a man no one else had discovered any trace of beyond a couple vague sightings at a cupcake shop and a movie theater? And if he did, what then?

He remembered the basement last June. He remembered Diedrich Keller bringing the butt of Linda's gun down on her head. He remembered struggling with Keller and the sound of the gun going off. He remembered the light in the Pride Killer's eyes quickly dimming as he died. He did not want to meet the man who killed Corinne Copley. He only wanted to know who he was and why he'd done it. The rest he would leave to the police.

"We appreciate your talking to us," Kyle said.

"Are you going to see the movie?" asked the man. "You paid for your tickets."

"No, thanks. We need to go somewhere else."

"Well, good luck to you," he said. And then, much to his relief, a small group of older women came into the theater. Six of them, out for an afternoon matinee, even though matinees were a thing of the distant past in movie theaters. They could still pretend and enjoy themselves.

"Good luck," he said again, turning his attention to the approaching women and glad to have the distraction. He didn't like talking about the young woman who'd been killed. He didn't like knowing he had probably seen the man who did it. He hated that he had not been able to help them catch the son of a bitch, and he hoped someone would—maybe this Kyle person and the woman he'd come with. Or maybe justice would have to wait for God. He had no doubt it would come then, no doubt at all.

CHAPTER Twenty-One

The movie sucked. Caroline's Say *was nearly two and a half hours of Caroline saying way too much. The jokes fell flat, the cast tried desperately to save the material, and it was all Corinne could do to keep from walking out an hour into it. But she'd paid for the movie, and nearly as much for popcorn and flavored water; plus she had the time to kill. So she'd sat through the drivel, tried not to laugh when she wasn't supposed to, and wished she had when the movie was clearly saying "Laugh Now!" Sorry, scriptwriter and floundering co-stars, not funny.*

It was about halfway through when she again had that sensation of being watched. There were only a dozen people in the theater — the reviews had not been kind, and it was a weekday afternoon. But when she turned around, trying to look like she'd heard something, taking in what she could see in the periphery of her vision rather than staring straight ahead at anyone, she saw only the smattering of people not laughing. Had there been someone in the seat four rows behind her? Why did she think that? There was no one there now and probably never had been. Just this feeling. She'd turned back around, endured the rest of the movie and gladly left, knowing she'd just lost two hours of her life she would never get back.

It was late afternoon and still very light. The clocks had changed three weeks ago and she loved having the extra hours of daylight. She also loved spring. She enjoyed every day of it while it lasted, knowing the stifling heat and the stench of summer would be here soon. She planned on having a wonderful time at dinner that night with just Gilda and a few friends. All thoughts of a ghost in a seat four rows behind her were gone. The stringy-haired man at the bakery, gone. Danger, gone. There were plenty of people on the streets, most of them seeming to be in the same good mood Corinne was in as she headed uptown on Eighth Avenue.

The man followed her out of the theater and watched her walk toward the corner. He'd ducked down into his seat just in time, almost being spotted by the girl. That was the only name he had for her, the only thing to call her: the girl. She was cautious, that one.

She had some kind of sixth sense. He knew all about that, having developed quite a strong one himself. You can't survive on the streets as long as he had without having ears, if not eyes, in the back of your head. He knew that's really where most of it came from: hearing what was around you. People heard someone coming up behind them. They heard a noise in their empty house. Sometimes they heard breathing in their ear, and by then it was too late. They turn. They stare. They cry out. Too late.

The girl also had not used her smartphone at all. The man found that most remarkable. Everyone had a phone in front of them or held up to the side of their head. Just as many had ear buds stuffed into their ears, blocking out the very hearing that might save their lives in a bad situation. Distraction worked to the advantage of people like him. Every magician knew that; every criminal, too.

He followed the girl along Eighth Avenue, wondering if she was finally headed home. He looked at his watch: three hours had passed since he'd first started following her. He was getting impatient and had decided he would act soon. He'd grab her purse and run if he had to. Sometimes when he did that people chased him, but he was very fast. He'd had to be. If you can't outrun what's chasing you, you get caught or you get killed. Either one was not an option.

He was relieved to see the girl turn left at 37th Street. Side streets were the mugger's friend. They weren't as bright and in the afternoon they were thick with shadow from surrounding buildings. There wasn't as much car traffic, and there were fewer people. Fewer people meant fewer witnesses. It also meant, statistically speaking, he was less likely to be chased. Good Samaritans felt emboldened when there was an audience and plenty of other people to join the pursuit or call the police. Side streets, not so much. No one wants to be gunned down or stabbed trying to save some old woman's purse. He'd discovered this through many experiments on his own. He followed the girl west on 37th Street, watching for his chance.

Then it happened. She took her phone out of her purse and began talking to someone. Perfect. She was not paying attention. She was off-guard. He hurried as quickly and as quietly as a rat, hoping to catch her mid-block, which is exactly what he did.

Corinne felt her phone vibrating in her purse. She'd ignored it all day, needing to keep up the ruse that she was at school. But now school was long over and she had not gone home. As expected, she saw her father's number on the screen. Guilt stabbed at her. She may be sneaky from time to time, but she was not a liar. She hoped he didn't ask her about school that day as she clicked the 'answer' icon and said hello to her father.

"Hi, Daddy," she said. Hoping to keep control of the conversation, she added, "I went to a movie after school, in case you're wondering. You can't have your phone on in movies, it's rude."

"Where are you, Corinne?" he asked. He knew she was going to dinner with friends.

"Don't worry, Daddy. I'm a big girl now."

"I didn't ask you if you were a big girl. I asked you where you are."

Corinne sighed, hoping he didn't hear her exasperation. Sometimes her father's hovering felt stifling. Her mother was much less of a worry-wart and wouldn't call Corinne at all, waiting until she got home that night to be filled in on the day's activities.

"Thirty-Seventh," Corinne said.

She thought she heard steps behind her, but she was halfway up the block now. And why wouldn't she hear steps on a street with other pedestrians? She ignored them and picked up her pace.

"That's a side street. I told you to stay off the side streets."

They talked for just another minute as Corrine kept walking. She heard the steps behind her again, but very close this time, and rapid. She swiveled around and saw him. The man from the cupcake shop. The ghost from the movie theater.

Skate Copley had just told his daughter that her mother was planning a trip to Boston when he heard Corinne talking to someone on the street.

"Excuse me?" she said, as if a stranger had asked for directions.

"Corinne? Who are you talking to?"

"Hey!'" she shouted. "Hey, that's my phone!" Then, to her father, "Daddy, he wants my phone! It's brand new!"

"Who wants your phone?"

"*Fuck you!*" she shouted.

"*Corinne,*" Skate said, his voice rising, "*give him your phone, just give him your phone.*"

"*Let go!*" she shrieked. And then a pop. A single loud pop. Not very menacing, but eternal.

Everything changed for both of them that night, April 23rd. Corinne Copley would never get older, never have another thought or say another word.

And Skate Copley would never recover. Even if he found the man who did this. Even if he turned his own world inside out, upside down, hung it by its ankles and shook out every last good thing from it. The one truly good thing had left him that night and the most he could ever hope for was satisfaction. Not justice — he knew better than to believe in that when all life's evidence witnessed against it. But someday, somehow, he might stop the sound that startled him awake night after night. He might put things right and finally, one more time, from somewhere far away, hear his daughter speak to him.

CHAPTER Twenty-Two

It was the second time in two days Kyle had stood on the street where Corinne Copley was killed. He and Linda had begun where Corinne had begun, then followed her steps from the beginning ... to this. A side street in Manhattan that looked like a thousand others. A vein running east to west across the city's grid. One way lay Eighth Avenue. To the other they could see cars driving south on Ninth Avenue, just a half-block ahead.

"So this is where it happened," Linda said. She stood, hands on hips, looking around at the buildings.

"Approximately," Kyle said. "It could have been two doors up or two doors down, but this is basically it, yes."

"And nobody saw anything?"

"Not anything that helped them catch the guy. But it was a man, we know that. We know it from the last conversation she had with her father. And we know it from two eyewitnesses who weren't close enough to give a detailed description."

"Really?" said Linda, surprised. "You didn't mention that."

"It was in the reports. A hot dog vendor who was pushing his cart ahead of us, and a woman about a quarter block back."

Linda thought about it a moment. Surely something they'd seen would have helped the police narrow down a list of suspects, maybe do a lineup.

"What did they see — or not see?" she said.

"The woman saw a short, skinny guy in a black or blue hoodie. She thought he had long brown hair, but she wasn't sure. Could have been shoulder length, could have been tied back. He pulled up the hood when he got close to Corinne."

"She saw that?"

"Again, yes and no. She said she wasn't paying attention."

"Let me guess, she was on a cell phone," Linda said, sighing.

"Of course," said Kyle. "She was on her phone, texting or whatever, and she happened to look up just when it all was happening. The guy goes rushing up behind Corinne, pulls his hood up, there's an argument — the one Skate heard — then the gunshot. The woman froze and watched as the man went running up to Ninth on the opposite side. She's the one who called 911."

"Well," Linda said, "if he ran up to Ninth, the hot dog vendor should have gotten a better look."

"He didn't," Kyle said. "He was too scared. The guy ran past him on the other side of the street and when the vendor called out, the guy pointed his gun at him and he ducked down. Figured he was going to get shot. He gave the same basic description as the woman: short, thin, dark hoodie and jeans."

"And a gun."

"A gun and a cell phone that belonged to a teenage girl he'd just shot in the head."

Linda was processing it all. It had been three years since the shooting. No one had been arrested. There had been no description good enough to put out more than a sketch of a man with a dark hood over his head and the lower half of his face showing. She knew the man was probably long gone, and possibly dead.

"Were there others?" she asked.

"Other witnesses?"

"Other cell phone robberies around the same time, the same week."

"They're not uncommon," Kyle said. "They still happen."

"I mean like this one, with deadly results, a gun."

"No, not that I know of."

"Then she seems targeted," Linda said.

"Yes, of course. That's what I've thought all this time. And that's the only way it will ever be solved. He didn't want just any phone. He wanted Corinne Copley's phone."

"Which means he didn't really want the phone at all."

Kyle stared at her. He understood now. "He wanted what was *on* the phone," he said.

"Emails?" Linda wondered. "But that wouldn't make any sense. Text messages? Her browsing history?"

And then he knew.

"Photographs," Kyle said. "He wanted the photographs."

"A teenager would have hundreds of them," Linda said. "How would he even know what pictures she had on there?"

"Because he wanted very specific pictures from a very specific time that day."

None of it made sense at that moment, but murder rarely did. How would the man know she hadn't posted the photos to social media already? How did he know they weren't automatically stored in the Cloud somewhere? He didn't; or he didn't care. Or, more likely, he'd been sent by someone who wanted the phone regardless of what Corinne may or may not have done with its contents.

"He was an errand boy," Kyle said, feeling certain. "That's why he followed her, why he sat through a movie. He could have taken anyone's phone, gone into the subway and snatched one from some half-conscious pedestrian listening to music on the platform with a train pulling in."

Linda knew he wasn't just making connections, he was taking leaps. Maybe there was truth to it, or maybe it was wild speculation. But it was better than the dead end she was about to tell him they had reached.

They were standing outside the barbershop Kyle had seen the day before. He wondered again if it had been there three years ago. Had no one inside heard the gunshot or seen the man running away? He knew the police would have questioned the barbers and whatever customers had been there, and he concluded it had probably been an empty storefront or another business now gone.

That is when he saw it. A flat-screen television mounted on the wall. The news was on. He couldn't hear it from outside, but he saw it clearly enough: Raul Sandoval talking to a reporter. He looked displeased. The media was dogging him now, following him from his home to his office, even staking out the gym where his wife went every morning.

"Look," Kyle said, pointing into the barbershop.

Linda walked up to the window and peered inside. Two barbers were busy cutting men's hair and chatting. They did not notice the strange man and woman standing in front of the window.

"What?" Linda said, perplexed. She knew little about Sandoval's indictment and the media firestorm around it, except what she'd seen on the Philadelphia news channels.

"The building," said Kyle. "Look where he is."

Raul Sandoval was standing in front of an apartment building. The one where he lived. The one where the guard had refused to tell them the names of its tenants.

The Centurion.

"We know who lives there now," Kyle said. "C'mon, we're going."

He took Linda by the arm and pulled her away, heading quickly up 37th Street. He let go of her jacket and kept walking.

"Where are we going?"

"To my office."

"But Imogene, what will she ... you're out sick for two days."

"She knows I'm not sick. And if this is the connection we've been looking for, she'll give me a month off when this is over."

Linda had only a vague idea what Kyle was thinking—that Raul Sandoval, the Manhattan District Attorney now under indictment in one of the biggest political blowups in the city's history, had something to do with Corinne Copley's murder. The thought seemed preposterous. He was a very successful man, in a world where most failed and those who succeeded had the scars to prove it. He was a prosecutor and a politician. He would not risk everything for a few pictures on a cell phone. It made no sense. But that, she knew, was where the truth to killing was often found — in the senseless and the rash.

They hurried to the corner and turned north. The Japan TV3 studios where just a few blocks away. Kyle's cubicle was there. Imogene was probably there. And among whatever evidence Kyle was able to find, the answers were there, too.

PART III

Corinne Speaks

CHAPTER Twenty-Three

Vivian LaGrange had been following the news closely for the last few months. She'd always assumed Raul Sandoval would get caught sooner or later, and she had to hand it to him for making it this far. He wasn't your average crooked D.A. For awhile she'd thought he might get away with his shady dealings and his crimes forever. Some people did. Meyer Lansky, one of the world's most famous gangsters, died an old man who was never successfully prosecuted. His was the mobster's dream, the criminal's fantasy, but he was one of only a handful Vivian had ever heard about who did not end up in a cramped prison cell or cemented beneath some metal beam at a construction site. Most of the crooks Vivian had known were forced into early retirement with their throats cut or bullets in their skulls, courtesy of their closest friends. She would be the first to admit her own fate was likely to be similar, but not yet, not now. She had risen to the top of the New York City crime underworld over the course of thirty years, and she had managed to stay there despite numerous attempts to topple her. The drug trade, in which Vivian had risen from dealer to impresario to undisputed queen, was as solid a career as one could choose. People always needed drugs: cocaine and heroin, with a surprising resurgence of pills, lots and lots of pills. And while she didn't need to supplement her income from narcotics, Vivian also took a slice from loan sharks throughout the city, serving as an ATM for the non-addicts. (The trouble with junkies was their tendency to die; it never hurt to have a second line of work.) Vivian had survived on her own wits, talent and ruthlessness, but sometimes with the help of men like Raul Sandoval. There were many like him — but not many as smart or as shrewd.

She hadn't expected an indictment against him so soon, but she should have. The United States Attorney Eleanor Duvall was an ambitious woman; bagging the District Attorney for

Manhattan would make her famous and assure her a swift rise up whatever ladder she was climbing. It would also make her a hero to those who liked watching big men fall, and Raul Sandoval was a very big man. Big and greedy, she thought, as she sipped sweet tea in her living room.

She'd only called on him for one favor, one time, but it was enough to entangle them in ways she regretted. He'd come through—he always came through when a suitcase of cash was on the floor in front of him—but he'd kept a bit of insurance for himself. She'd been a fool to give it to him and now she wanted it returned. The girl's phone. The girl who was not supposed to be killed for it but had been. An innocent child. A national news story. An ace in Raul Sandoval's hand, should he choose to play it, and Vivian didn't doubt he would once he found himself faced with a deal from the federal prosecutor.

"Leon," she called out, using the remote to turn off the television. She'd seen enough of Raul Sandoval proclaiming his innocence, attempting to deflect attention with cries of racism and political vendettas.

Leon Carter was her lieutenant, her right-hand man. He'd been with Vivian since he was just a street soldier running errands for her and driving her around town. Then, one sunny afternoon outside a restaurant in the Bronx where she'd gone to talk peace with her late, great rival, Jorge "George" Restrepo, Leon had saved her life and taken a bullet for her as they got back into the car. Leon survived with nothing worse than a slug in his shoulder; George Restrepo did not. He'd claimed innocence and insisted it had been a terrible accident of timing—wrong place, wrong time—but Vivian knew who was behind her attempted murder and within a month George was found in the East River with two mouths: the one he'd lied with, and the one an assassin had added to his throat with a serrated knife. Business was business.

Leon came in from the balcony where he'd been smoking. Vivian hated cigarette smoke and only permitted it outside her ninth floor apartment to keep Leon at heel when she needed him. She did not trust luck, and she worried that the one time Leon was on the street sucking a cancer stick was the one time they would get past him, up the stairwell and into her living room. "They" could be anyone; there were old rivals, and enough up-and-comers who wanted to make a name for themselves by putting an end to Vivian LaGrange. Leon Carter helped her make sure that didn't happen.

Leon was a big man, six-feet-four and tipping the scales at nearly three hundred pounds. He dressed impeccably in suits and ties, and he had the face of a cherub, if cherubs killed for a living.

"Yes, Boss," he said, coming back in from the balcony.

"Wash your hands," Vivian said. "They smell like smoke."

She always told him this after he'd had a cigarette. He crossed behind her to the island kitchen that opened onto the living room. She could hear water running as he cleaned the tobacco smell from his hands.

Vivian was a good looking woman and Leon had been tempted on several occasions to initiate something inappropriate between himself and his boss. She was somewhere in her early fifties—she never said, and she did not celebrate birthdays. It was a very ripe age for someone in her line of work. She wore it well, remaining thin and as elegant as someone with her background could be. She'd had acne as a teenager, that was evident from the pockmarks on her face, but she covered it well and had enlisted the help of a very skilled plastic surgeon and a top-flight dermatologist to all but eliminate the scars. Her hair was dark red, her eyes brown, and when she smiled it was impossible to believe she'd ordered the deaths of men and managed to stay ahead of every law enforcement officer who had ever fantasized bringing her down. Leon knew that when the time came, Vivian would go down on her own terms.

He finished drying his hands on paper towels, dropped them in the kitchen trash can and came back into the living room.

"Remind me again," Vivian said, "where the body of the little snake can be found?"

It was a trick question. The "little snake" she referred to was the meth head who'd stolen the girl's phone. The street slime Leon had inadvertently sent on a mission he should have taken care of personally. One phone call led to another, and a job reserved for someone skilled was outsourced to a moron with a gun.

"Nowhere, Boss."

"How many parts was he cut into?"

"Many," Leon said. "Spread far and wide."

"And never found," she said.

"Never found."

She finished her tea, then sucked on the last piece of ice. She set the glass down on the coffee table.

"It's time to speak to Mr. Sandoval again," she said.

Leon didn't like this but knew it was coming. He was a fiercely loyal lieutenant, that went without saying, but he was also human and his own survival came to mind now and then. If Vivian LaGrange found herself in a prison cell, Leon Carter could not be far behind. He wished none of this had ever happened, but he couldn't voice his concern. After all, it was his fault the little street thug had been sent on a mission any halfwit could have accomplished without bloodshed.

"Please call the number," Vivian said, referring to the phone number only she, Leon and Raul Sandoval had. It connected to a phone Sandoval used for only one purpose. Vivian knew this because she had given it to him. Did the number even still work? She hoped so. It had been at least two years since she'd made use of it, but she knew men like Raul kept every avenue open, every line of communication available.

"Tell him I'd like to have a conversation with him," she continued. "Face to face."

"Yes, Boss," Leon said. He took his cell phone from his jacket pocket and headed back to the balcony to call the secret number.

"Oh," said Vivian, just as Leon was about the close the sliding glass door behind him. "And tell him to bring the phone."

"Yes, Boss," Leon said. Two words he'd repeated thousands of times over the ten years he'd been with Vivian. She had been very good to him. She'd taken him with her as she rose to the heights, freed him from the streets and brought him to penthouses. But something told him her time was running out, that the great Vivian LaGrange was about to have a run of bad luck, and bad luck in this business was usually the last luck someone like Vivian ever had.

He'd had offers of his own, of course. Quite a few, to the tune of hundreds of thousands of dollars, if only he would say, "Yes, Boss," one last time while he put a bullet in Vivian's head. He'd resisted, mostly out of loyalty, but also with the knowledge that whoever paid him for the job, praising him and thanking him with a handshake, would probably be waiting behind the next corner to make sure Leon never told anyone what he'd done or for whom.

There were other numbers he could call, numbers Vivian did not know about. Numbers to those very men who'd been waiting patiently for years to strike. He took a deep breath, dialed the phone number to Raul Sandoval's secret phone, and made a note to himself to dial another. Soon.

CHAPTER Twenty-Four

Kyle could have done some online searching at home, but he focused better at his office. That's where he spent time researching stories and following leads for Imogene, and that's where he took Linda after leaving the storefront on 37th Street where they had just seen Raul Sandoval on a barbershop television standing in front of the Centurion.

Imogene was there, but thankfully occupied in Leonard "Lenny-san" Baumstein's office. Lenny was the New York station manager, reporting directly to his bosses in Tokyo. Fifty-four years old, tough but fair, he'd been in the business as long as Imogene and she respected him. That was important. Imogene had found herself near the bottom of the ladder she'd once perched atop because of her quick mouth and her readiness to use it, telling a few bosses what she'd thought of them and finding herself having to look for another job. Tokyo Pulse was the last stop on the career train for her. Or it had been until the Pride Lodge murders. That's when she became a serious asset. Once she was a hit beyond the 3:00 a.m. Tokyo crowd, who'd considered her entertainment when she was clumsily covering financial news (something she knew less about than she knew about speaking Japanese), her bosses instructed Lenny-san to make her more visible, more of an attraction. He put her on the New York City general beat, covering politics, culture, and the occasional homicide, and nearly three years later Kyle marveled she had not taken an opportunity elsewhere. But she loved the job, the people and Kyle. She loved being a celebrity in Japan, and was even planning a trip there in July at her employer's insistence. It seemed a toy maker was putting out an Imogene-san doll and they needed her for promotion. (Kyle had been needling her to take him, but no commitment had been made.)

He knew she was talking to Lenny-san about the Sandoval story. It was huge, the biggest thing in New York dirty politics since a City Councilman was photographed passed out from a night of booze and ecstasy at a water sports party — the urination kind. Sandoval was going down, no one doubted that. Eleanor Duvall would not stake her reputation and career on charges she could not prove. But how would it unfold? And who would Sandoval take with him as he tumbled toward incarceration?

Linda looked nervously at the corner office. She could see Imogene, whom she'd met on a few occasions, talking animatedly behind the closed glass door.

"She uses her hands a lot," Linda said, watching Imogene.

"She's expressive, that's for sure." Kyle had his eyes on his computer screen, looking through news stories from three years earlier.

"Does she know we're here?"

"Let's hope not. And let's hope we can find out a few things and get out of here before she's finished with Lenny-san."

They'd stopped for coffee and bagels at the 38-Nine Deli. Skate wasn't at work that early. Niz was behind the counter, and his wife Meriem was stocking shelves. None of his daughters was ever in the store; Niz considered it inappropriate for them to be seen there. That's what he had Skate and two other employees for.

"Just a few days more," Niz said, handing the bag with coffee and bagels to Kyle.

"A few days to what?" Kyle had said.

"You know. The anniversary, with Skate's daughter."

Niz Ramani had been at work the night Corinne was killed and he was well aware of what happened. That's why he'd hired Skate, to offer compassion and give the man something to focus on as his life spiraled into despair and brokenness.

"Skate tells me you're going to find the killer," Niz said.

Kyle had blushed, embarrassed and worried that Skate would think this, let alone tell anyone. He was looking into the case, that's all. He knew better than to make promises, and he had not made any. Only that he would retrace events from that day and see if there was anything the others had missed. And there was: the seeming coincidence that Raul Sandoval lived in the building where Corinne and Lydia had stopped for photographs. It probably meant nothing, but assuming it was meaningless was exactly why no one had followed up on it.

Linda turned back to the desk and watched as Kyle did a news search. The mayor three years ago was Michael Bloomberg. Plenty of news stories about his handling of the city, his conflict with the unions, his installation of pedestrian walking spaces and his efforts to turn the city into even more of a playground for the rich than it already was.

"I'm not seeing anything," Kyle said. He'd looked for anything that stood out, any big stories occurring within a month or two of Corinne's murder.

"Maybe it's not something that ever made it into the news," Linda said.

"Then we're screwed."

He was about to give up and think of some other avenue, another line of questioning, when he saw a headline in the New York Times. April 28th, five days after Corinne's murder.

District Attorney Disbands Grand Jury in Triple Homicide.

Raul Sandoval was still new to the job then. As Kyle began to remember it, this had been a big story. Three people were found murdered in an apartment in Greenwich Village. Bound with duct tape and shot execution style, each one receiving a bullet to the back of the head. Two men and a woman. The only witness was a baby that had been spared and left crying on the floor beside its mother's body.

… D.A. Raul Sandoval has determined there is insufficient evidence to proceed with charges against Jordan LaGrange in the

gruesome murder of three adults in Manhattan's Greenwich Village. LaGrange, twenty-six and the son of reputed crime queen Vivian LaGrange, is reported to be leaving the country within the next few days. LaGrange had maintained his innocence since the bodies of Michael and Lucinda Maffei were discovered April 3rd by a neighbor who smelled a foul odor coming from the apartment below her. The neighbor, who declined to be interviewed for this story, babysat for the Maffeis and entered with a key they'd given her. She found the couple dead in the living room, along with an unknown second man later identified as Paul Maffei, a younger brother. The infant was released to Child Protective Services and placed in foster care. Sandoval has offered no comment, saying only that he did not have the evidence required to pursue homicide charges in the case.

Linda read the item over Kyle's shoulder.

"Wow," she said. "You think this has something to do with it?"

"Probably not," said Kyle. "But the timing is right. I mean, there's nothing else even remotely connected to Sandoval in the timeframe we're looking at."

"This could be a wrong turn," Linda said. "It might have nothing at all to do with him. And who is Vivian LaGrange?"

Kyle turned off his computer. He wanted to leave before Imogene came out of Lenny-san's office. If there was a connection between Raul Sandoval, the murders in the Village, this Vivian LaGrange woman and the death of Corinne Copley, it would be the biggest story the city had seen in years.

"Did you ever see the movie *Scarface*, with Al Pacino?" Kyle asked.

"Who hasn't?" Linda said.

"That's Vivian LaGrange, but much more subtle." He grabbed his coffee and the bag that still held two bagels. "Let's go."

"Where to?" asked Linda, getting up and rolling her chair back to the empty cubicle she'd borrowed it from.

"It's time to talk to Robin Dietz."

"Who's that?"

"He's the detective who worked Corinne's murder. The one who passed confidential information to Skate."

"But if he gave him confidential information and we go to the precinct, don't we risk getting him in serious trouble?"

"We're not going to the precinct," Kyle said. "We're going back to the apartment and I'll call him from there. He may not even be in, but I'll keep trying until we can get him alone, in private. I want to run these things by him and see what he says."

"What if he thinks there's nothing there?" Linda said. They were headed out now, down the row of cubicles toward the stairs.

"Then we keep digging," said Kyle. He pushed the stairwell door open and held it for Linda.

"You know," Linda said, following Kyle down to the first floor, "if someone was willing to kill Corinne Copley –"

"Don't forget three dead bodies in the Village," Kyle said over his shoulder as they descended.

"Right. If someone with a link to a mass execution in the Village was willing to kill a teenager, they're probably willing to kill you."

Kyle did not lose a step, did not hesitate a beat.

"I can't worry about that," he said.

"But what's the connection?"

Kyle stopped, almost at the first floor door. He turned back and looked at Linda.

"The phone," he said. "The connection is the phone."

He offered no further explanation as he pushed through the glass door and hurried out of the building.

CHAPTER Twenty-Five

His mother was the first person to call him Cricket, when he was three years old, maybe four. Unfortunately for Billy Thatcher she wasn't the last; the name stuck and he'd spent the next twenty-five years being called Cricket, like some fucking bug. She said it was because he jumped around all the time when he was little and made funny noises, "Like a fucking Cricket, just like one, get Mommy the pipe on the dresser. And a beer." He tried to bury the name. He told people he was Billy, and if he was feeling especially elegant he'd say his name was William. But somehow they always knew, somehow they found out, and he had never been able to shake the name. "Cricket do this," and "Cricket do that." They made him jump, just like the fucking bug his mother named him after.

He was in a bad mood. Things had gone wrong with the girl. He should've known not to bring a gun. You don't need a gun to steal a phone from a kid. But these were dangerous streets and he almost never traveled without a pistol in his pocket. A small one his last girlfriend used to carry until he pushed her off the roof. Kept the pistol, kept the cash she'd made that day from six blowjobs to guys coming off the buses at Port Authority, and shoved her off the roof of the Exeter Hotel. The room was in her name, they didn't know who he was and couldn't prove anything anyway. He told the cops Suzie had gone up there to smoke a rock and the next thing he knew there was an ambulance coming and a lot of chatter in the hotel lobby. Place was full of drunks, junkies and meth heads, just like Suzie, but a body landing six flights down onto the sidewalk was enough to excite even the comatose. They never pinned anything on him and after some minor league interrogation they cut him loose. He hadn't wanted to kill her; he'd just wanted to teach her a lesson. But things got out of hand and this kind of shit happened sometimes.

Like shooting the girl on 37th Street. Maybe he was just impatient. He'd followed her half the fucking day, for chrissake! From the cupcake joint into the movie, then after sitting through that godawful piece of shit he followed her uptown. Cricket wasn't more than a quarter block behind her, waiting for the right opportunity. He knew he couldn't fuck this up. He knew the orders came directly from Leon, even though they'd been filtered through Sidney. Leon was top-tier, working for V, as everyone called her. Sidney was next rung down, then a big drop to people like Cricket. He was surprised they'd trusted him and figured someone was in a hurry. He also figured he had to come through if he ever expected to work his way up even a little. Doing a job for Sidney, who was doing a job for Leon, who was doing a job for V, was a very serious responsibility. He could not fuck this up.

And then he had.

It was the way she talked to him, the way she resisted, like he was a bug. He'd waited hours for her to just take her fucking phone out of her purse and hold it up, that's all. Just put it where he could grab it. It was weird, the way she didn't use her phone that day, like she was avoiding someone or she didn't want to be bothered. He had no idea she was skipping school and hiding out — that's why she wasn't using her phone — he learned that on the news the next couple days after it happened. He also saw how hot the story got. This was some big shit. Part of him wanted to bask in the glory, anonymously, of course, and part of him wanted to get the fuck out of town, as far and as fast as he could. This was some heat, some pressure. How was he supposed to know the whole killed-for-a-cellphone thing was gonna go huge? Some other kid in a Kansas parking garage got shot for one, too, and now it was a big deal on all the sorry-ass news channels that needed something to fill the time. He got caught up in it, that's all, wrong place right time kind of thing.

He looked up from the corner of 42nd Street and Ninth Avenue where he'd been standing for the past fifteen minutes waiting for Leon. He still hadn't been paid for the job and Leon was bringing him the three grand they'd promised. He'd given Sidney the phone the same night he stole it, but no word back after that. Until this morning, when Leon himself called and said he'd done good, "Good job, Cricket." How the fuck Leon knew his name was a mystery; Sidney must have told him. He was flattered. He'd had to leave the Exeter Hotel and settle into a men's shelter after the whole Suzie fiasco. Fucking men's shelter, can you believe that? Drunks, faggots, sorry-ass losers. He was only there for a little while, he knew that, they knew that, and as soon as he had the money from Leon he was going to take a bus to Philly and step back a bit.

He saw the black sedan glide toward him. He didn't know the driver, looked like a fucking chauffeur, with the fucking cap and jacket. High class shit. Leon was in the passenger seat. Cricket recognized him. Everybody recognized Leon. Giant motherfucker. Makes you nervous just to look at him. But he was smiling and he waved, a little hello wave like some pussy, some happy-day shit. The car pulled up to the curb in front of Cricket and Leon motioned to the back seat.

Cricket hurried to the car, started to open the back door, and froze. There was a woman in back. Who the fuck? She smiled at Cricket and patted the seat next to her as he opened the door and climbed in.

"You must be William," she said.

William? She called him William? How the hell would she know his name? And who was she? His mind was racing, flipping through memories and images as fast as any computer, then it hit him. Oh. My. God.

"Are you …?"

"Vivian," she said. "Vivian LaGrange. I'm the one who asked you to take care of this little … inconvenience. Well, I asked that Leon to take care of it, and here we are."

The car pulled away, headed toward the Lincoln Tunnel.

"I was worried," Cricket said, staring at her. He could not believe he was in the back of a town car with the most successful, and most dangerous, criminal mastermind to control the dope trade in New York City in probably thirty years. And a woman! Damn!

"I wanted to personally thank you," Vivian said. "And to pay you. I'm sure you'll appreciate that."

His eyes widened as she opened a leather satchel and removed a large envelope. He assumed it was stuffed with cash. Vivian handed it to him, not commenting on his trembling.

"It was an accident," he sputtered. "The gun, I mean. I carry one, you know, for safety, but it kinda went off by itself."

"When you pointed it at her head, you mean?" Vivian said.

Leon and the driver had been silent the whole time.

"I didn't mean to point it at her head, that's what I'm saying."

Vivian was silent a moment, then said, "Don't worry about it, William. Everything will be fine. You don't have the gun with you now, do you?"

"No! No! I threw it in the river, like Sidney told me."

"Good boy," she said. Then she made the slightest eye contact with the driver. He pulled over near the corner of 37th and Ninth, just down the street from where Cricket had accidentally put a gun to Corinne Copley's head and accidentally killed her.

"Enjoy your hard earned money, William," Vivian said. She opened her car door and slid out, just as another car, a dark blue Mercedes, pulled up behind them. Cricket had no idea it had been following them.

"You're leaving?" Cricket said, glancing back through the rear window at the Mercedes.

"I'm a very busy woman." She turned back to Cricket. "Thank you so much again," she said, then closed the door.

Cricket watched through the back as Vivian LaGrange walked leisurely to the car behind them, got into the passenger seat and pulled the door shut.

And then he heard the car lock click as the driver locked him in.

That was odd, Cricket thought. He looked down at the envelope of cash in his hand.

"I'll take that," Leon said.

Cricket turned and saw Leon staring at him.

"I don't understand," Cricket said.

Leon pointed a gun at him and said, "Of course you don't."

Then he understood perfectly well.

Cricket .... William ... Billy Thatcher, street hoodlum, sometime drug addict, full time loser, was never seen again.

CHAPTER Twenty-Six

The Stopwatch Diner was located just a block from Penn Station, the *other* train stain in Manhattan (Grand Central being the most famous and the only one of the two saved by preservation from the travesty committed on Penn Station, which was now more of an underground strip mall than a city treasure). The diner had been in business for thirty years and was, by its own proclamation, a landmark. Started by brothers Sid and Allen Murray, it was now run by Sid's son Richard. Allen's family had taken a buyout in the early 2000s, which had spared the clan the sort of acrimony that tore other families apart under these circumstances. Richard Murray could be found at the diner six days a week, from 7:00 a.m. until nearly midnight. His two marriages had not weathered the business as well as his family had, and he really didn't have anyone to go home to. No wife number three, no kids. The Stopwatch was his everything.

Kyle and Linda had been here before when she visited the city. It was also where Danny had learned why his nemesis, restaurateur and vulture capitalist Linus Hern, hated him so much. (Danny had been hired at Margaret's Passion to replace Linus's then-boyfriend Sal, who subsequently slipped back into drug addiction and threw himself off the 59th Street Bridge, for which Linus blamed Danny and made a serious but failed attempt to destroy him.)

They were seated quickly. The diner was bustling even this late in the afternoon. It was, after all, a landmark, with its giant "Stopwatch Diner" sign hoisted over the front door's exterior and its racing motif—checkered flags, giant photos of race car drivers spewing champagne in simulated orgasms as they celebrated long-ago wins, and another enormous clock in the design of a stopwatch taking up a large section of the back wall.

Detective Robin Dietz had agreed to meet them there. As Linda had suspected, he did not want to meet them at his precinct. He was the insider who had taken pity on Skate Copley (fueled, certainly, by his own desire to see the killer caught) and passed to Skate sensitive information that could get him into serious trouble with the Department. The reports, the autopsy, the witness statements. All had come from Dietz, and slipping them to the dead girl's father would be a breach of the most serious kind.

"Why do you think he gave Skate all that information?" Linda asked, sipping coffee while they waited.

Kyle had wondered that himself, but concluded it was Dietz's way of relieving his guilt at being unable to solve the case. He could only do so much; he had a job to go to every day, in a city that never ran short on murders, no matter how well a series of Republican mayors and tough-on-crime police chiefs had cleaned up the city. He'd been able to let Skate know someone would never forget what happened, someone would always want the same answers Skate wanted.

"I think it was his way of giving Skate ... hope, I guess, or at least a way to distract himself from the grief. I mean, look at him: from serious success in the financial industry to working at a deli a block from where his daughter was killed. Divorced, no other children. Living across from the bus depot. He needed something to keep going, and Detective Dietz gave that to him."

Linda was about to continue the conversation when she saw him walk in. She knew what he looked like from his photographs online—she'd checked on her phone on the way to the diner. Quite the decorated police officer, this one, and not a bad looking man, if she were giving fair appraisals of men. Five-feet seven or thereabouts, jet black hair he kept gelled back. No glasses. He was wearing a dark sport coat, not a suit. She waved at him (Kyle had his back turned to the door) and he waved back, heading quickly to their table.

Linda slid out of the booth and offered her hand. "Detective Dietz, good to meet you. I'm Linda Sikorsky."

"Also a detective," Kyle said. He started to get out of the booth as well but Dietz motioned him to stay seated.

"Retired," Linda added. "New Hope, P-A. Homicide. But twenty years was enough for me."

"I hope it'll be enough for me," Dietz said. "I've got another six to go, then we'll see. May I?"

Kyle nodded yes, then slid over so Robin Dietz could ease into the booth beside him.

No sooner had Dietz sat down than the waiter walked over.

"Nothing for me, thanks," Dietz said, and the man moved on.

"So," said Dietz, getting to the point. "I'm glad you're doing this for Skate—he told me all about you, or as much as he knows—but I'm not sure how I can help you."

"We think we found something," Kyle said.

"In the reports?" Dietz replied, lowering his voice as if someone might hear him and know he'd broken departmental rules.

"Yes and no," said Linda.

"It's what was *not* in the reports," Kyle clarified.

"I don't understand."

"I believe she wasn't killed for her phone. At least not the phone itself. I think she was killed for what was *on* her phone."

"Like, emails or texts?"

"More likely photographs."

Dietz turned sideways and looked at Kyle. "But those would have been uploaded to the cloud or something. Nothing's just on a phone anymore."

"It is if you set it to be," Linda added. "Kristen—that's my partner—"

"Wife," Kyle said. *Partner* still sounded like someone you opened a business with, and in light of gay couples being able to marry it became even more vague. He was pleased when

Dietz showed no sign of disapproval, even though it wouldn't matter if he had.

Linda continued: "She has her phone set to prevent uploading. She doesn't want her photos or documents or anything else floating around up there ..."

"Clouds are servers," Kyle said.

"I know what clouds are," Linda replied patiently.

"So you think she had photos on her phone that she didn't put on Facebook, didn't share with anyone ..."

"She was skipping school that day," said Kyle. "She didn't want her parents to know, so she didn't post anything. And she didn't upload her photos to a cloud."

"You can verify this?"

"Not without the phone, but I can call her friend Lydia and I will wager heavily that Corinne Copley did not casually let her photographs be shared with a cloud or a server or anywhere else outside her control."

It made sense in a way. It was easy enough to believe Corinne Copley had been a random victim, someone chosen for the opportunity, but they'd known all this time she was followed. From the cupcake shop to the movie, then on toward the restaurant for dinner. Kyle and Linda were not the only ones with this information. But the trail—and the case— had gone cold once the killer ran off with the phone. He'd even had the presence of mind to turn it off so it couldn't be traced or tracked. And it did not have a kill switch.

"Any idea what these photos might be?" Dietz asked.

He's taking us seriously, Kyle thought. "I think it was a picture, or pictures, she took in front of the Centurion."

"The apartment building?"

"Yes. That one. She and Lydia stopped there so Corinne could get a picture of them in front of it. It's a very famous building. And that's where this ties together, I think."

Dietz pondered it a moment, then said, "How so?"

Kyle had no good answer. "I really don't know," he said. "But when we were back at Thirty-Seventh Street, where

Corinne was killed, I looked at a television set in the barbershop there and I saw ..."

"Raul Sandoval," Linda finished. "Standing in front of the Centurion almost shoving a reporter with a microphone stuck in his face."

"Raul Sandoval," Dietz said.

"The District Attorney."

"I know who he is. I just don't see what he has to do with anything."

"That's what we have to find out, and where you could possibly help us," said Linda.

"I don't understand."

Kyle leaned in and said, "Inside information. Nothing you can't find a way to tell us without bending the rules too far, but you're with the Department. I think there's some connection between Corinne Copley's murder and a triple homicide in the Village three years ago, a couple months before she was killed."

"I remember that case, who doesn't?" said Dietz.

"We think," Linda said, "that Raul Sandoval dropped the case against Jordan LaGrange as a favor, or some kind of payback for Vivian LaGrange."

"And Corinne Copley knew about it?" said Dietz, startled.

"I don't know," Kyle said, exasperated. "I just don't know. But there's a connection, I'm sure of it. Somehow Corinne's death is connected to Raul Sandoval, who's connected to Vivian LaGrange. And there in the center is the phone. I just can't stop thinking that."

"And you want me to poke around," Dietz said.

"More like *listen* around, that's all," Linda said. "Maybe ask a few innocent questions, see what's been heard."

"It was over three years ago."

"I know," Kyle said. "I just don't know what else to do. I can't ask Sandoval anything, and if I went to this LaGrange woman I'd probably end up in a landfill."

Dietz looked at his watch. He'd been there for twenty minutes and needed to get on with his day.

"Listen," he said. "I don't want to promise anything. And I hate to disappoint you, but I probably will. This idea of yours is a little ... out there. But I'll ask around, discreetly. I'll see what might have been missed."

He slid out of the booth then, quickly shaking each of their hands.

"I hope you can help Skate with this," he said. "He's a good man, really. It's so wrong, what happened to his daughter, and what's happened to him since then. But you have to be prepared for disappointment. It's the way the world really works."

"Thanks," said Kyle, his spirits slumped but not fallen. He believed he was onto something and he was going to pursue it, with or without help.

Detective Robin Dietz gave them a last wave and headed out of the diner.

"Now what?" Linda said. She could see the hint of resignation in Kyle's face, but also the determination.

"Now I think we eat," Kyle said. "I'm starving. We can get something to take back for Danny. I don't plan on cooking tonight, sorry."

"No problem," said Linda. "I wouldn't expect you to." And then she raised her hand, motioning for the waiter to come back.

Outside the Stopwatch Diner Robin Dietz, Detective Third Grade, stood watching the traffic, remaining close to the building to stay out of the pedestrian flow while he thought about the meeting he'd just had with Kyle Callahan and the retired cop from Pennsylvania. He didn't like where it was going, didn't like it one bit. He'd given Copley all the information to distract him. The man had been unrelenting, calling Dietz every day, wanting to know what was being done to find his daughter's murderer. He'd done vigils and put up reward flyers, and shown no sign of stopping if there was nothing to divert him. Better to feed him useless reports and statements from witnesses who saw next to nothing, let him obsess over it privately, chasing ghosts in circles until he gave up, exhausted.

Now this.

He walked around the corner out of sight. He took out his cell phone and called Leon Carter. Whether or not Leon would know what to do wasn't his concern. This was Leon's problem — and Vivian's — not his. He wanted as far away from this as he could get. With Sandoval going down it might be time to start looking at early retirement destinations, somewhere with no extradition treaty to the United States.

Leon picked up on the second ring.

CHAPTER Twenty-Seven

Robin Dietz, Detective Third Grade, sat drinking his second Jack and Coke of the night, his ass warming the fourth stool from the door at Mackey's Star Bar. There were no stars at Mackey's, no one who came close to being a celebrity outside the few square blocks surrounding the place. Mackey's was the definition of a neighborhood dive in Ridgewood, Queens, where Robin lived. He knew the bartenders, and they knew him. He knew the dozen or so regulars who never seemed to leave, sitting at the bar if he happened by on a Sunday afternoon, and there when Mackey's closed its doors at 3:00 a.m., the bartender having lingered an extra hour just to get them out. He'd never understood how they could drink that much without blowing out their livers, or how they paid for it, but he could understand why: life was something you had to numb yourself to get through, at least for these people. The regulars at Mackey's numbed their every waking moment and most of their sleeping ones.

Robin wasn't that bad, but he knew the impulse well. He'd known it since his his cop father was killed on the job after twenty-three years, just a few months from retirement. Wasn't that always the way? Just about to get out. Just about to start living the life they'd dreamed about and waited for and trudged toward; then some piece of shit had an especially bad day, walked into the precinct where Murray Dietz was about to go off shift, and started shooting. The dirt bag died with seventeen bullets in him; Murray only took one to the heart. Bang. Perfect. Dead before his body hit the floor.

That was five years ago, coinciding (in a not-so-coincidental way) with Robin's slide into booze, gambling and pussy. He couldn't decide which had cost him more, but he knew which one had caused the most trouble — the trouble he was in now, the trouble that had him calling Leon Carter after he'd met with the foolish snoop Callahan and the dyke. She was a looker, he'd give her that. But she was also dangerous. Robin Dietz knew a tough character when he met one, and Linda Sikorsky was tough. She didn't have to say much; it was the way she moved, the way she looked around, observing everything. He'd only been surprised she wasn't carrying a gun, but maybe she had it in her purse.

His gambling accelerated after his father's murder. The money Murray left his only son didn't help; Robin could now wager hundreds of dollars on a single horse, or blow through a thousand dollars in an hour at a craps table. It had taken less then a year for the money to be gone. By then Robin was too addicted, too hooked on the ecstatic rush of the bet, and he fell further and further in debt. Bookies don't like being owed money, and it wasn't long before Robin found himself talking to Marty Persaud. Marty was well known and well connected. He told Robin he'd get him five grand by dinner time. Then it was another five, and another, until Robin found himself owing Marty fifty thousand dollars. Not chump change, and enough to get you killed if you squelched on your debt.

That's where Leon Carter came in. Somehow Leon (or, much more likely, his boss Vivian LaGrange, the one they called V) learned about Robin's debt and his position as a homicide detective. There was this little matter of Vivian's son Jordan being suspected in a triple execution and having someone on the inside would be most helpful to Vivian. Within a few days Robin's debt magically disappeared. Marty Persaud stopped asking for his money back, and even offered Robin a few thousand at no interest for Christmas that year, something special for his special customers. Robin had the distinct impression Marty feared for his life, should he not treat Robin with utmost care and respect. But Robin knew the score; he knew the only thing that stood between life and his sudden death was a woman who had people killed as easily as anyone else ordered flowers for Mother's Day. And that woman expected a significant return on her investment.

So Robin had given her information about the murders in the Village, the ones for which her son was widely considered responsible. He'd told her, through Leon, everything he knew as soon as he knew it. He even tampered with evidence, making a pair of sunglasses Jordan LaGrange had dropped at the scene disappear into thin air. Jordan wasn't the brightest young man and it was best for everyone that he now lived in Bermuda. But times had been tense three years ago. Vivian had been worried. She'd done what she had to do, which included getting Raul Sandoval into her pocket, and now she was at another critical juncture. Sandoval was almost certainly going down. Vivian would do everything in her considerable power to make sure she didn't go down with him. Robin had no doubt that "everything" might include killing the District Attorney, but that would be as high-profile an assassination as Vivian had ever ordered, and a last resort.

He ordered his third drink and sipped it on the fourth stool at Mackey's Star Bar where the only stars were dimmed beyond hope, so faint they could not be seen by the naked eye. Robin felt like one of them, and as he looked over at Maggie, whose last name he doubted anyone at the bar knew, he understood how she could sit there drinking hour after hour. She was one of those regulars who never seemed to leave. She was somewhere in her late thirties, appeared to be about twenty years older than that, and right now, between drinks, she looked pretty damn good. Booze, gambling and pussy. He'd take it all.

"Hey," he said, sliding over onto the empty stool next to Maggie. "I seen you here a bunch of times. My name's Robin. Can I buy a lady a drink?"

She smiled at him. It had been awhile since anyone called her a lady. Then she lifted her hand—that's all it took—and the bartender brought her another bourbon, straight. It just might be her lucky night.

CHAPTER Twenty-Eight

Kyle had ordered takeout meatloaf from the Stopwatch for Danny's dinner. Danny could eat any night of the week at Margaret's Passion—they owned the restaurant—but like many people who worked in eating establishments he had little desire to take his meals there. They were excellent, of course, but they were how he made his living. A nice plate of "Grandma's Mystery Meatloaf" from the Stopwatch was just fine with him.

Danny was eating his dinner at their small kitchen table while Linda and Kyle kept him company. Neither of them were hungry after the meal they'd ordered once Detective Dietz left. Smelly and Leonard had been fed as soon as Kyle got home; it was a habit he'd developed shortly after moving in with Danny: a hungry cat is an annoying cat. Better to feed them and keep them quiet than have them meowing through a conversation. Or weaving in and out between his feet, sometimes tripping him, as he tried to accomplish anything in the kitchen. (He'd also taken to giving them treats early in the morning when he was at his computer; Danny disapproved, but Kyle told him it was the only way to shut them up. Smelly was particularly demanding, and if he just gave her a handful of tasty tuna fish nuggets she would let him get on with his work.)

Kyle and Danny were planning another trip to Florida in the fall. They'd gone to Coral Springs once already to visit Margaret Bowman. Her departure from New York, from the restaurant that bore her name, and from Danny's daily life had been particularly hard on him. Margaret had plucked him from near-obscurity at a competing restaurant twelve years ago. She's seen something in him, as both an outstanding restaurant manager and, were she to admit it (which she readily did), a surrogate son. She and her husband Gerard never had children. Then, fifteen years ago, Gerard was killed in a freak accident outside the restaurant, hit by a taxi as he stepped to the curb to stamp out his cigarette. Margaret had told her husband many times that smoking could kill him, but she had never imagined it would be like that. She'd been alone after his death, and once she had Danny she felt like she had a family again, even if it was only the two of them.

Danny had a family of his own. He had his parents in Astoria and two sisters who lived out of state. And he had Kyle, with the cat Leonard as a bonus. "A twofer," Danny told him. He was about to turn fifty-eight in a few months and the passing of time weighed on him. Would he someday be Margaret, losing Kyle to a freak accident or an untimely death? Would he find himself alone in his old age? These were morbid, completely unnecessary thoughts, and he sometimes wondered if he should make his own appointment with Peter Benoit to talk about them. Or maybe he and Kyle could go together, a sort of couple's massage for the mind.

"What do you think Dietz can do?" Danny asked. They'd filled him in on their meeting with the detective.

"I don't know," Kyle said. "Probably nothing. But he has access, obviously."

"Obviously," Linda said. "You know, passing that information to Skate Copley was highly unusual."

"Not something you would ever do," Danny said, "being the woman of law and order that you are. By the book and all."

"No, I wouldn't. I investigated dozens of deaths in my years on the Force, quite a few of them homicides, and I never gave privileged information to the families. It's a serious breach of protocol."

"Corinne Copley's murder wasn't just any murder," Kyle said, immediately regretting the way it sounded. No one's murder was normal; every survivor of a loved one's death considered the trauma unique. "What I mean is, it was huge news. It turned into much more than the story of a teenager robbed and killed on a Manhattan sidewalk."

"I remember it," said Linda. "I remember seeing it on the morning news shows. I don't remember interviews with the family, though."

"There weren't any," Kyle said. "Skate wouldn't talk to the media, and neither would Jennifer Copley, his ex-wife. It was national news anyway. Grieving family members are a nice-to-have but not necessary. I know from experience."

"So Dietz took pity on Skate," Danny said, finishing his meatloaf. "He broke the rules. And if he hadn't, you wouldn't have the leads you followed today."

"We don't have any leads," Kyle said. "At least not from the material Skate gave me."

"Right," said Danny. "You followed her footsteps, you spoke to the guard, you saw Raul Sandoval standing in front of the building" – all information Kyle had given him while he ate his dinner – "now what?"

"I'm curious about these murders in the Village."

Danny knew about those, too. No one had ever been charged and there had been rumors for years that something very dirty had kept it that way.

"I thought you wouldn't be dealing with any murderers this time," Danny said. He was acutely aware of the aftershocks of Kyle's last encounter with a killer. Six months of therapy had just begun to help.

"I'm not interested in the killers," Kyle said. "Actually, I think I know who that was."

"Jordan LaGrange," Linda said.

"Yes. And he's in Bermuda from all accounts."

"Who is Jordan LaGrange?" Danny asked.

"The son of Vivian LaGrange."

"Well," said Danny, "that answers my question. Now who the hell is Vivian LaGrange?"

"Think Scarface in a little black dress," Linda said darkly.

"Oh my God," said Danny, sliding his plate away. "Please don't tell me this is some underworld thing."

"Three people shot execution-style in the Village," Kyle said. "A crooked D.A, some kind of serious involvement with a criminal she-boss. Of course it's an underworld thing."

"I don't like it and I won't have it," Danny said. The force of his words startled Kyle. "You're going to get killed one of these days, Kyle. You almost got killed the last time. As did I! You didn't mean to shoot Diedrich Keller. And if he'd had his way all three of would be dead. I'm telling you, as your husband and your life mate and your best friend, I will not have this."

Kyle and Linda were silent. Danny had never put his foot down before, not through the Pride Lodge killings or the Pride Gallery murders or even the worst of it, the Pride Killer, left dead on the basement floor while Kyle stood over Diedrich Keller's body in shock. But that, he insisted, would be the end of it. No more close encounters with madmen. And now this. A woman capable of killing from a distance, killing with an order and by someone else's hand.

"I'm not looking to confront Vivian LaGrange, if that's what you're worried about," Kyle said.

"I don't think she'd let you get close enough to do that," said Danny. "I'm worried about her having you killed long before you got anywhere near her."

"I thought you didn't know who she was."

"The name rang a bell, Kyle. Like Genovese or Gambino, but much worse. I remember her now, I remember reading about her. They even did a special on one of those investigative TV shows. She's never been charged with anything, but they think she's had dozens of people killed."

"'Death in High Heels,' I think that episode was called. I saw the show."

"So no," Danny said. "You will not go near her. You will not alert her in any way that you're interested in her. Look what she did to those three people in the Village."

"That was her son," Linda said.

"Oh, well then," said Danny. "That makes all the difference. Now excuse me, I've enjoyed the meatloaf, thanks to both of you, but I'm going to the bedroom now. It's been a long day and I just want to watch the news."

Danny got up from the table and left them, clearly upset.

"I'm worried he doesn't like me anymore," Linda said. It was an exaggeration, but there was a kernel of truth to it. She would not be surprised, nor would she blame him, if Danny had come to resent her for the danger she and Kyle welcomed into their lives.

"He loves you," Kyle said. "You and Kirsten both."

"I think that will turn to hatred if anything happens to you."

"Nothing's going to happen to me."

Linda paused. "So are you going to stay away from Vivian LaGrange?"

"Yes, I am. *We* are. "

"We'll wait for word from Detective Dietz?"

"I didn't say that."

"I don't know what our options are then," said Linda.

Kyle took Danny's fork and speared a piece of broccoli Danny had left on his plate. He popped it into his mouth.

"We're going back to the Village," he said.

"What are we going for?"

"*Who,*" Kyle said. "Jordan LaGrange may have escaped indictment in these murders, but it doesn't mean he didn't do them. I want to speak to the woman who found the bodies."

"The upstairs neighbor who didn't want her name used in the news."

"That's her. One of the police reports said she changed her statement, and it gave her name: Louise Ridgley. You can't stay anonymous on the record."

"What changed about her statement? Did she say she didn't find the bodies after all?"

"Oh, she found them," said Kyle. "And she saw who did it. At least that's what she said the first time. Then she conveniently forgot—or someone helped her forget."

This was news to Linda. Kyle had not said anything to her about a witness changing her testimony. Considering this involved Vivian LaGrange's son, she was surprised the witness was still alive. The more she learned about the LaGranges, the less she wanted to know, and the further away she wanted to stay.

She glanced at the clock on the stove. It was almost seven o'clock and she had not called Kirsten since the morning.

"Excuse me," she said, getting up from the table. "Time to call Wifey."

Kyle smiled up at her. "Does she know you call her that?"

"No, and she never will."

Linda left Kyle sitting at the table. There was more uneaten broccoli on the plate—Danny didn't like the vegetable. Kyle slid the plate over to himself and began finishing it. He had to think, to formulate questions for Louise Ridgley, the neighbor they were going to see in the morning, the one who'd smelled corpses decomposing downstairs and who had suddenly un-remembered what she'd heard and seen two nights earlier. They would speak to the woman tomorrow. Then they would speak to Detective Dietz again. And finally, somehow, they would make their case to the authorities—whoever they were. Considering how high up the corruption went, Kyle wasn't sure they could trust anyone.

CHAPTER Twenty-Nine

Vivian LaGrange had slept well. She'd seldom had reason not to, except for that short time when her son Jordan was the prime suspect in a completely needless triple murder. A meeting with Raul Sandoval had taken care of that, as had a minor bit of witness intimidation. Witnesses, Vivian knew, were not hard to intimidate. Pretty much everyone, with the exception of the rare martyr, prefers life over preventable death, and all they had to do to avoid it was recant testimony or suddenly forget what they'd seen.

Her conversation with Detective Robin Dietz had not troubled her. She wasn't worried about him talking to the police—he was the police—and his mother, God bless her, was still alive and vulnerable. Dietz knew that even if he vanished into the Witness Protection Program, changing names and living out his life in quiet fear somewhere in Idaho, his mother would not escape. He knew, too, that Vivian had no scruples when it came to protecting herself and everything she'd worked for. One dead mother wasn't much to her.

She was also not particularly worried about this meddlesome man, Kyle Callahan, or his woman friend. Dietz had told her about them when he called. He'd been nervous; he was always nervous, and Vivian knew how to leverage other people's anxiety. She had remained beyond suspicion in the girl's murder for three years. No one outside the very small circle of Sandoval, Dietz, Leon and the dead drug addict who'd pulled the trigger knew Vivian had anything to do with that tragedy. And now, what? She was supposed to worry that some nobody from a TV channel and his retired detective sidekick were going to uncover what they had kept so well hidden all this time? No, Vivian told herself, no one is going to come along and ruin everything out of simple *curiosity*.

She should have had the father killed long ago. He was the one who wouldn't let go. He was the dog with the bone. Were it not for him, there wouldn't be some nosy nobody looking into things that could get him killed — and would, if it came to that. But she'd seen no harm in a grieving father with a useless obsession, so she'd let Skate Copley keep looking and looking, knowing there was nothing for him to find.

She was much more concerned with Raul Sandoval and his willingness to trade her for some kind of limited immunity. He would never get full immunity; Eleanor Duvall did not hunt whales only to let them go. But she would surely give him something, some promise that he would not spend the rest of his natural life in a prison cell if he gave up someone like Vivian. She was the whale's whale, the mountaintop. She knew this, too, and she knew she might have to silence the biggest threat she'd ever faced. It wouldn't be easy, but nothing in her life ever had been.

As for the meddling Callahan fool, he should be easy to dissuade. She picked up her phone and dialed Leon. He lived in a one-bedroom apartment two floors down from Vivian, paid for as a necessary expense. If she'd wanted to be completely safe, she would have him living in her second bedroom, but that was just too much.

"Yes, Boss," Leon said when he answered. He sounded fully awake at 7:00 a.m. He always sounded fully awake. A man like Leon must at least *appear* to never sleep. If Vivian's enemies knew he slept, they would know he could be taken.

"I have a small errand," Vivian said, sipping her second cup of coffee. There would only be two on any given day.

"Anything you need, Boss."

"Just promise me it will be handled professionally," Vivian said. She didn't need to repeat this but she always did. The girl's murder had been a terrible mistake, committed by an idiotic creature sent by a third-level soldier. A delicate matter handled most indelicately. It would not happen again.

"I can put Cecilia on it," Leon said.

He could tell by Vivian's pause she was impressed—and slightly threatened. Cecilia Ramirez was an up-and-comer in the fast lane, and Vivian saw much of herself in the young, ambitious woman. She'd considered taking Cecilia directly under her wing, to keep her close if nothing else. Women like Cecilia were formidable, and dangerous. Vivian knew this— she had been one of them.

Vivian thought of telling Leon this didn't need someone as accomplished as Cecilia, then she thought better of it. She didn't know where Callahan's meddling might get him, or what the witness might reveal. Better to have someone very sharp taking care of things.

"Fine," Vivian said. "Cecilia it is. But tell her she cannot kill anyone without my direct approval. I know how she loves to end people's lives."

"You got it, Boss. So what do you need?"

"I need her to follow someone, quickly."

"How soon?" Leon asked.

"This morning."

She knew where Kyle Callahan lived—information is extremely easy to come by these days. And she knew he was moving rapidly, putting things together that should never have been connected. She guessed, rightly, he would not stop to catch his breath, and the sooner she had Cecilia following him, the better.

"Call her," Vivian said, finishing her coffee. "Now."

CHAPTER Thirty

It was Friday, another day closer to the anniversary of Corinne Copley's murder. There was no deadline to what they were doing, but there was a sense of momentum Kyle did not want to lose. He worried that if he stopped now, if he even slowed down significantly, he would not be able to get back the steam he'd lost and the whole thing would just collapse: no murderer found, no motive, and no end in sight for Skate Copley's nightmares.

He was also aware of the importance the case had taken on in his own life. It had been days since he'd thought about Diedrich Keller dying on the floor of his own townhouse, life vanishing from his eyes as quickly as a thunderclap. Would Kyle's worries, and his own bad dreams, return if he solved Corinne's murder? Will this all have been just a distraction that kept him from his own truth, his own despair at becoming a killer himself?

"You're not a killer," Linda said.

The words startled Kyle, as if she'd read his mind. They were sitting at the kitchen table finishing their morning coffee. Both had dressed; both had passed on breakfast when Danny offered to make it. There was a sense of impending finality to the morning, the indescribable but distinct feeling they were nearing a critical juncture.

"I don't know what you're talking about," Kyle said, looking away to hide his alarm.

"I know how troubled you've been, Kyle," she said. "About Keller's death. I know you think it makes you like him . . . like *them*."

"I don't think that at all," Kyle lied.

"It's perfectly natural. I remember the first time I took someone's life—killed someone, because that's what it is, truly, we killed someone. I felt horrible, Kyle. I felt like I had no right to end another human being's existence, but it was a very similar situation."

"As a cop," Kyle said. He was looking at her now.

"Yes, as a cop. It was my second year on the Force, and there was a robbery, a jewelry store. I got there just when the robbers were running out of the store."

"Like your dad," said Kyle.

He knew the story of Linda's father, how he'd gone to the corner grocery store for milk for Linda's cereal (something for which she carried irrational guilt most of her life), and encountered a robbery in progress. He was off-duty and unarmed, and in a split second he was bleeding to death, hit in the neck by a stray bullet as the robbers shot it out with policemen arriving at the scene.

"Yes and no," Linda said. "I had a gun, and I shot back. As a matter of fact, the one I hit and killed was a woman."

"Really?" Kyle didn't know why this surprised him.

"Women can be bad people, too, as you now know with this Vivian LaGrange. Women can be very bad people. Anyway, I didn't mean to kill her. It just happened, in a flash, Kyle, just like the gun going off in Keller's basement, the one that could have killed you as easily as it killed him. You had the upper hand for the instant it took, that's all. You're not a killer. You're not a murderer. And frankly—please don't resent me too long for saying this, but we're very close friends now and I think I can—it's time for you to let go of the self-pity."

Kyle set his coffee cup down. "Self-pity?"

"Yes, Kyle, there's an element of self-indulgence in thinking you must be a bad person because you killed someone. I'm all for therapy, really, don't misunderstand me. But the time comes to move on . . . from everything in our lives. Our childhoods, the deaths of our parents, the loss of nearly everyone we love and care about if we live long enough. Life is one long letting go, Sweetie, and some things are better let go of than others. Having a gun go off and killing a vicious serial killer who would have left us all dead in his basement sounds to me like something to let go of pretty easily, and quickly. So go ahead, take a deep breath and let it pass."

Goddam her, she's right, Kyle thought. He'd examined and explored his life in analysis with Peter Benoit for six months. It was time to take the weights he'd found and lift them off, cast them away. In truth, he had used the crisis to look at other, more hidden things in his life, especially his relationship with his father. It wasn't easy knowing your parent didn't like you. They loved you because they had to, it came with the instructions, but they didn't have to like you and Bert Callahan had not liked his son and only child. *So fucking what?* Kyle thought. *You're fifty-six years old. He's been dead for twelve years. So. Fucking. What.*

"Thank you," Kyle said. "I needed to hear that. And it spares Danny having to tell me! Now let's get out of here. I know how much you like riding the subway."

"You know where she lives?" Linda asked.

"Oh yes, it's in the statement."

"The one she changed."

"That would be the one. So let's go."

Kyle stood up, taking both their empty coffee cups. He hesitated a moment, then said, "Detective Linda, I have to ask . . ."

"Yes?"

"You didn't bring the gun with you, did you?"

Linda couldn't tell if he was asking because he hoped she'd brought her gun or because he didn't want it anywhere near him. It was the gun he'd killed Diedrich Keller with. It was also her father's gun, his service revolver from his days as Military Police in Vietnam.

"No, I didn't bring it," Linda said. "Kirsten wouldn't let me. But she's getting pretty damn good at shooting it!" She winked at him, then got up from the table. She was wearing long pants and had been since her arrival. It hid the ankle holster and the small pistol she kept strapped to her leg. Kyle would never know it was there unless he had to, and if that happened he would be glad she'd brought it.

"Let me tell Danny we're leaving," Kyle said. "He's in the shower."

Kyle headed into the bathroom to say goodbye for the morning and let Danny know he would call once they were on their way back from the Village. The two men stayed in touch more often now, ever since Danny almost died on a gurney in Diedrich Keller's killing room. It could seem a little obsessive to an outsider, but to Kyle and Danny it was a lifeline they held closer these days. They had rarely been apart in almost nine years together, and now if one of them was going from point A to point B, they always sent a text on arrival. *Made it. Safe and sound. See you at home.*

Linda was waiting by the door when Kyle came out of the bathroom.

"Does she know we're coming?" Linda asked.

"Louise Ridgley?" Kyle said. "No. I think an element of surprise helps."

"What if she's not there?"

"Oh, she'll be there. She became agoraphobic after the murders. I found a follow up interview with her online. If you can call it an interview. She wouldn't talk, so the writer came up with a few paragraphs about her. 'Life in the Shadows' or something like that. She hasn't left her apartment in two years."

Linda suddenly had visions of walking into a hoarder's home. Agoraphobia and hoarding were two very different syndromes, but the idea of not leaving your apartment for two years left a lot to the imagination.

"Let's go," Kyle said, opening the door and holding it for Linda. He was beginning to wish she'd brought her gun after all. Something about this visit seemed dangerous, and the people they were closing in on—if they were right about who was involved in the death of Corrine Copley—were definitely lethal.

CHAPTER Thirty-One

Raul Sandoval was accustomed to watching the sunrise. Most mornings he was up well before it, and he would sit in his apartment office glancing out at the slowly growing light while he worked on cases, wrote speeches, and mapped the course of his life. He'd been doing it since he was a teenager. *Ambitious* was a word used to describe him since childhood. "That boy is ambitious," his uncle would say as Raul started another small business selling trinkets from their garage. Or, "Raul is a very ambitious young man," his teacher would say, with just a slight undertone of concern—not all ambition was benign, and for some it required a ruthlessness the teacher probably saw in him. There were others like him, many others, leaders in business, innovation and the arts. People who were driven to succeed from a very young age. But, to his mind, there was only one Raul Sandoval, one human being on the planet with his particular destiny. And now he saw that destiny threatened. Everything he'd worked for from the age of ten to this moment, jeopardized over one bad choice, one entanglement he should have avoided. It was his weakness for cash that did him in—might do him in, unless he could find the angles he needed to escape paying this highest of prices. If he could just buy some time, divert some attention, point those seeking to destroy him in another direction. But how?

He'd dreaded getting the call he got last night. Leon Carter called him on their secret number, the one connecting to a phone Raul kept in his desk drawer. Gloria didn't come in here. She was not interested in his business and his career beyond what they provided her, which was enough to keep her nose out of where it did not belong. There were many things Gloria didn't know and would deny knowing if she did. Like his involvement with Vivian LaGrange, the briefcase filled with cash she'd personally given him, and the damage control that led to a young woman's death. Raul felt badly about Corinne Copley. He'd been horrified when he saw the news reports of her murder and knew the phone he had in his possession is what she'd been killed for. But he did not feel badly enough to tell anyone, to ruin his own life as penance for the actions of a street criminal.

Leon called him during his favorite television show, *Cooking with the Masters*. He knew the phone in his desk was ringing because he had it forwarded to his cell phone, the one never out of arm's reach. Gloria was watching the show with him and ignored the Batman ringtone. She was used to Raul getting calls at all hours of the day and night. She kept watching while he got up and headed into his office, closing the door behind him. The caller ID told him it was the *other* phone, the one only three people knew about, the one that had not rung in the two years since his last contact with Leon.

"What?" he'd said abruptly, closing the office door behind him.

"She wants to talk to you." It was Leon's voice; Raul would never mistake it for anyone else's. There was a predatory sound to it, a threatening tone that was present no matter what was said. Leon Carter could say "I love you" and sound like he was about to strangle you.

"So put her on the phone," Raul replied. He could feel his palms begin to sweat.

"In person," Leon said. It was not a request.

"That's not possible. You've seen the news. Vivian certainly has."

"You mean you're the lead on every fucking station," said Leon.

He had a point. "Exactly," Raul said. "There's heat, a lot of it. Maybe she should have Eleanor Duvall disappeared."

It was an attempt at humor that failed.

"V doesn't have people killed," Leon replied flatly. "I don't know where you get these ideas, Mr. Sandoval."

A shiver ran through Raul. When last they'd spoken Leon called him *Raul*. Now it was *Mr. Sandoval*. Frighteningly formal.

"When?" Raul said.

"Tomorrow morning would be good."

"Where? You know I have reporters following me. The scum."

"Just go to Clarette's for breakfast at ten o'clock. Ask for their private room."

Clarette's was a very upscale restaurant in the Flatiron District, and a very secluded spot to meet someone you did not want to be seen with.

"I'll be there," Raul said, noticing the nervousness had moved into his bowels.

"And bring the girl's phone," Leon said.

Raul was about to protest, to stall for just a few moments while he thought things through, when the line went dead.

Surely she would not kill him in a restaurant. Maybe he should take Gloria with him. He could tell her everything and ask her to help him stay strong, to go with him while he put a stop to this madness before it went any further.

It can't go any further, he thought, hearing it as if someone else were speaking to him. *It's gone as far as it can.*

That wasn't true, of course. It *could* go further. It could go all the way to Raul's death. But what cards did he have left to play? None. He had the phone, that was all. He'd never looked at any photos on it—the phone was locked and Raul had not been about to give it to someone to try and break its password. Come to think of it, why would Vivian LaGrange want it? *Maybe because you couldn't unlock it and she can, asshole*, he thought. Or maybe she really was planning to put an end to Raul Sandoval and this was the only memento she would have of their brief time together.

He heard a knock at the door.

"Raul, you're missing the best part," Gloria said, her face close to the doorframe. "They're having a cook-off."

The best part. The words struck him as funny. He'd be getting to the best part in the morning, sitting in a private, hidden booth at an elegant restaurant, waiting to see what Vivian LaGrange had in store for him. Either the best was yet to come, or the worst.

CHAPTER Thirty-Two

Louise Ridgley lived on the third floor of a walkup on Greenwich Street, just at the lip of Greenwich Village and within sight of what had once been St. Vincent's hospital. St. Vincent's had served the neighborhood for over 150 years, including acting as ground zero during both the AIDS crisis and the aftermath of 9/11. A fence across the street from it, now gone, had been covered with photographs and handwritten cards commemorating the thousands who'd died when terrorists flew passenger jets into the World Trade Center. When it was closed and slated to be turned into luxury condos, hundreds of New Yorkers from the area and beyond protested fiercely. It was history, it was comfort, it was a place they had known all their lives. But like all places we know all our lives, it, too, was destined to vanish eventually.

Louise had several strong aversions, quirks most people call phobias: she did not ride in taxis, subways or airplanes; she only took empty elevators, and only when she absolutely had to get from one floor to another and there were either no stairs, or too many to climb; and she had not stepped on a sidewalk crack in forty years.

The dead couple had lived in the apartment below her. Louise had not been especially close to them, but friendly, and they had asked her several times to babysit and even given her a key to their apartment. It was the key she'd used to enter when she had not seen or heard from them in two days and a foul odor began seeping up through the bathroom vent.

"You said she hasn't left her home in two years. How do you suppose she makes money?" Linda asked, as she and Kyle stepped up to the building's intercom.

"Maybe she telecommutes, or maybe she invested wisely."

"How old did you say she was?"

"I didn't," Kyle replied, just before pressing the buzzer for 3D.

He had not given Louise Ridgley any warning they were coming. He had also not been certain she would be here, but considering her refusal to leave her home there weren't many places for her to be.

"Do agoraphobics talk to strangers?" Linda asked.

Kyle detected some teasing in Linda's tone. Good. Somebody had to keep a sense of humor, at least in reserve. Investigating murders could get deadly serious.

Kyle rang the buzzer a second time.

"Who is it?" a woman's voice said sharply.

Speaking into the intercom, Kyle said, "My name is Kyle Callahan. I'm a friend of Corinne Copley's father. And I'm with Detective Linda Sikorsky. We're looking into the death of his daughter."

"I don't know any Corinne Copley," she said.

"She was the teenager killed three years ago for her phone. Not long after the death of your neighbors."

There was a long pause.

"I have nothing to say," Louise said. "Please go away."

"Will you please talk to us?" Linda said in her most soothing tone. "Just for a moment? For Corinne?"

Kyle thought they'd just been cut off and left standing on the front steps when the buzzer sounded to let them in.

"That's a good sign," Kyle said, grabbing the front door and opening it before it could lock again.

They walked up to the third floor, unsure which way to go, when they saw an apartment door open slightly and a woman peer out. They walked carefully, slowly, to Louise Ridgley's apartment door. She did not open it further.

"I told the police what I knew," Louise said, speaking through a three-inch crack. Kyle could see the chain still drawn across the door.

"It will be three years soon," Linda said, using the same comforting voice she'd used with too many loved ones she'd had to tell their daughter was dead, or their husband had been found shot outside a bar.

She could see Louise's face soften just a bit, then the woman said, "I remember now. Such a sad story. But I don't see any connection, and I don't remember anything. I told the detectives that. You can go away now."

Linda eased forward. "Ms. Ridgley—"

"Miss."

"Miss Ridgley, I'm Detective Sikorsky. I'm retired, actually. I'm working this case as a favor to an old friend who suffered a terrible loss."

She's very good with the lies, thought Kyle.

"We think the same people who were responsible for the deaths of your neighbors are somehow involved with Corinne Copley's murder and we just want to ask a few questions."

Louise shut the door. Kyle was about to declare their mission a failure when the chain slid across and the door slowly opened again. Louise Ridgley may have made herself a shut-in for two years, but she kept herself presentable. She was dressed in slacks and a pullover, not the stained sweat suit or wrinkled housecoat one might imagine of an agoraphobic. Her hair was long, red, and tied back in a ponytail. She looked to be in her forties as she squinted several times at them. She did not step back or invite them in.

"I told the police I didn't see or hear anything," Louise said. "I found the bodies, that's all. And isn't that enough?"

Kyle knew he had to be very careful. It was like approaching a mouse, or a skittish cat. One wrong move or word spoken too forcefully and the animal would flee.

"Miss Ridgley," Kyle said, "I was looking at the police reports, and it appears you changed your statement."

Louise stared at them. It was a critical moment. She would either continue talking, or slam the door in their faces.

"I misremembered, that's all."

"Of course," Linda said. "I misremember all the time. We're just wondering . . ."

"If you could tell us what you *thought* you saw the first time."

"It doesn't matter what I thought I saw," Louise said. "I didn't see it."

There was some logic to her words. If she had not seen what she originally said she had, then what was the point in describing it?

The facts: Louise Ridgley first told police she had heard a commotion downstairs two nights before she found the bodies. The Maffeis lived alone with their baby in the apartment. Louise was making hot chocolate; she did this every night at precisely 11:00 p.m. It helped her sleep. She was in the kitchen, which has a window onto Greenwich Street. She heard shouting beneath her and tried to ignore it – Michael and Lucinda Maffei were known to argue loudly sometimes, but nothing that ever required police intervention. There were three loud booms, which Louise attributed to the prevalence of violence on television, or perhaps the video games Michael Maffei was known to play during most of his spare time. Then nothing. Louise went to her window, cup of hot chocolate in hand, and that's when she saw them: a man she later described as looking very much like Jordan LaGrange, and a second man wearing a cap that hid his face. Something about the men frightened her and she quickly moved away from the window. She gave it no more thought until the awful smell and the discovery of the bodies, with little baby Jessica sitting on the floor beside them, staring into space and sucking on an empty baby bottle. She never did cry; such a good baby. This is what she told the police, and the story she'd stuck to until Leon Carter showed up.

Kyle wasn't sure where to take the conversation next when Linda said, "Miss Ridgley, we're not here to cause you any trouble. And we will not tell anyone what you tell us. This is just between us."

Her tone remained comforting, woman to woman. Kyle could see Louise relaxing just a little. She glanced out the door, behind Kyle and Linda, as if making sure no one could see or hear them.

"I didn't see anything," she said. "Ghosts, really, two men in dark clothes, hurrying off to a car somewhere. I didn't go to the Maffeis because we weren't close, except, well . . .   I babysat for them sometimes. They kept to themselves. I keep to myself. It wasn't until I smelled them . . . you know, decomposing."

"It must have been so terrible for you," Linda said. "But tell me, please, just between us, was there a reason you misremembered? Did someone help you forget?"

Kyle could see tears welling in Louise Ridgley's eyes. He knew then what a burden it must have been for this fragile, frightened woman to have carried this with her for three years, two of them locked inside her house.

"He was big, that's all," Louise said.

"Who was big?" said Linda.

"The man who told me to forget. He was very tall, very calm, and very certain I would need to remember things differently if I wanted to stay alive."

There it was. The witness tampering, the death threat.

"Did he tell you his name?" asked Kyle.

"Of course not!" Louise said. "He didn't come to the apartment, either. He came up behind me when I was walking home from the grocery store. It was a very short conversation, but very clear."

Kyle was thinking it through. The murders were three years ago. Louise Ridgley had withdrawn to her apartment two years ago. She'd had a year of moving about freely, or as freely as someone like Louise ever moves about.

"Why did you decide to stay in your home?" Kyle gently asked.

"Because I like it here," Louise said.

"I mean, why so much later?"

Louise said nothing. She was calculating the risks in her mind. She has already said too much. She had told them something she had never told anyone. Would the big man come back? Was he watching her now from across the street? Had he been watching her all this time? The thought of it made her tired. She was so weary, so worn from living behind her front door and paying people to do everything for her, to cut her hair, buy her groceries and clean her laundry. So very tired.

In a voice so low and weak Kyle had to lean in to hear her, Louise said, "I saw him with the policeman."

"Who?" said Linda. "The tall man who threatened you?"

"Yes. I saw him with the detective. I was in the city having lunch with my friend Eloise. Poor woman died last year from stage four ovarian cancer. I couldn't even go to the funeral, since I don't go anywhere."

"You were having lunch with Eloise," Kyle prodded.

"Yes, at Delores's Café, on Christopher Street."

"I've been there, it's a nice place."

"Gone now, like everything else," said Louise. "It's a bank, or maybe a nail salon. Why bother going anywhere when all the places you went to are gone? So we're sitting in a booth, and I looked over and saw him. The big man. Just the back of his head, mind you, but I recognized his voice. It's not a voice you ever forget. He didn't see me. Neither of them did."

Linda felt her stomach churn as she anticipated what they were about to hear. She said, "Who was the policeman, Miss Ridgley? Who did you see the big man with?"

"Why, that Detective Dietz, the one who took my statement. I could tell something was off when he seemed pleased that I changed it."

It was as if a hole had just opened in the sky and lightening had struck them in Louise Ridgley's hallway. *Detective Robin Dietz.* The man who'd given Skate Copley all this information . . . for what? To distract him? To keep him looking in the wrong direction, or going in circles until he just gave up? And how much danger had they put themselves in? How much danger had they put Louise Ridgley in? Dietz now knew what they knew. He knew they were closing in, and if he was not a killer himself, he was doing business with some who were. Stone cold killers. People who murdered teenage girls for their phones and slaughtered their victims in apartments with babies watching, leaving the bodies to rot and bloat.

"We've stepped into a nest of vipers," Kyle said to Linda.

"Excuse me?" said Louise.

"Nothing, Miss Ridgley," Kyle said. "Thank you so much for talking to us. We'll leave you alone now."

Kyle, too, wondered if the apartment was being watched. It was a ridiculous thought, given how much time had passed. But Dietz was onto them, and he knew it was mutual. It was best to get away from here as quickly as possible, to let Louise Ridgley vanish back into her seclusion and hope no harm came to her.

Louise said no goodbye; she simply closed the door and disappeared back into her apartment.

"Let's get out of here," Kyle said, turning and hurrying back down the steps.

"Where to? Shouldn't we go to the police now? The *good* ones?"

"And how will we know who those are? No, I want to go back to the office. I have an idea."

Linda didn't like the sound of that. Kyle's ideas had a tendency to get them into dangerous situations, as they had again. But she trusted him, and she had not come up with any alternatives, not yet anyway. They hurried back toward the subway station.

Cecilia Ramirez had watched them enter the apartment building from a half block away. She knew they were talking to Louise Ridgley. She had no way of knowing what the woman told them, but she could guess, and every guess she made was unpleasant. Judging from how quickly the pair hurried away she assumed they had been told something they should not have been told. They would have to deal with the Ridgley woman sooner rather than later, but for now Cecilia would head back uptown on the same train, possibly in the same car, keeping close to Kyle and Linda and determining the best way to stop them.

CHAPTER Thirty-Three

"Smile," Vivian said, then she quickly snapped a picture of herself and Raul sitting in a booth at Clarette's, one of her favorite restaurants in the City. Not many of the high-end establishments served breakfast and she was in the mood for the eggs Florentine, hollandaise on the side.

"I thought you didn't like photographs of yourself in public," Raul said. He was in a sour mood and decidedly on edge. He knew that people who had private meetings with Vivian LaGrange were sometimes never seen again. Like that piece of shit street punk who stole the girl's phone. God only knew where his body was buried, probably in several locations.

"This is a special occasion," Vivian said. "And besides, Raul, you're the one who doesn't like pictures of yourself—at least not with me. Or don't you remember?"

He remembered too well. It had been his agitation at knowing the girls had captured them on film, if that's what you even called it anymore. He was the one who worried, the one who wanted the camera. (Goddamned smartphones, they're everything now, computer, camera, even a phone!)

"I was doing you a favor," Vivian said, as if reading his mind.

Raul looked around them before responding. Clarette's catered to a clientele of leisure—no one was in a hurry here. If you had to eat quickly, you went to a diner. If you were a person of means, you ate at a place like Clarette's and let those who wanted your time wait for it. There were only a half dozen people in the small main room, all of them preoccupied with their own thoughts and their own conversations, no doubt about power in its many forms. Raul's favorite form of power was money. It's what made his life so enjoyable, but also what landed him in a booth on Friday morning talking to the woman across from him.

"I was thinking of us both at the time," Raul said. "If it got in the news that Vivian LaGrange—or should I call you V?—was seen coming out of the Centurion with Manhattan's District Attorney, just when her son was under suspicion for murdering three people, it might not look good."

He laughed, but Vivian could tell it was the chuckle of a nervous man. She liked that. Nervous people were often frightened people.

"I've been told," Vivian said, finishing the last of her eggs Florentine, "there's some curious man looking into this."

"Into what?"

"*This.* The Copley murder. Those stupid, awful killings in the Village—Jordan will never set foot in this country again, by the way."

"Good," said Raul. "He's a monster."

"Yes, he is, and I say that as his mother. But this man, Kyle Callahan, and a woman friend of his, they've been to see the Ridgley woman."

Raul's eye's widened. "Really?"

"Really. We should have had her removed a long time ago."

Removed, Raul thought. What a clinical way to put it.

"It's too late now," Vivian continued. "It would only draw unwanted attention if she suddenly went missing. But I'll think of something."

Not, *We'll think of something.* She was clearly finished with him. Raul began to feel played with, as if he were a wingless bird and Vivian LaGrange was a cat. He did not like it, and relished the thought of his Plan B, now percolating back to the surface. He hadn't wanted to need it, hadn't expected to ever put it into action, but things were getting very, very hot and he did not enjoy the heat. A cool Spanish breeze was more to his liking, somewhere off Spain's Costa Dorado.

"In the meantime," Vivian said, "I'll take the phone now."

That was it, the reason they were meeting. Raul had known this and he'd brought Corinne Copley's phone with him. The battery had died three years ago, and it looked like a useless piece of handheld machinery.

"There's no charger," Raul said, sliding Corinne's phone from his jacket pocket.

"I'll find one," Vivian replied, taking the device and holding it in her hand. It wasn't heavy. It wasn't even impressive, given the advances in technology and the *coolness* of everything now. It appeared . . . old. And there, near the power button, was a stain that looked like dried blood.

"All that trouble for *this*," Vivian said. She even felt a quick twinge of sorrow—for the girl, for her family. She prided herself on never harming innocent people (this did not include belligerent witnesses, rivals, and family members killed for the necessity of making a point).

"You're the one . . ." Raul started to say.

"No, *you* are the one," Vivian said, stopping him. "You are the scared little district attorney who told me we'd just been photographed. You are the one who asked me to get the phone, somehow. None of it thought through, none of it planned. Impulse is a dangerous thing, Raul, but that's what you ran on that day."

"You could have said no."

"I'd just paid you to get my son out from under a grand jury investigation. I, too, can act on impulse, and my impulse that afternoon was to keep you happy."

"So we're both culpable."

"No," Vivian said coolly, "we are not. You asked for the phone, I got it for you. And you never even looked at it, did you?"

"I couldn't. I didn't have the password."

"So you don't know if there are pictures of us on it?"

"No."

"And you didn't know if those pictures you were so worried about were already out there, shared with her friends, or up in some cloud somewhere."

"They weren't, obviously."

"You're a lucky man, then," Vivian said. She put the phone in her purse, wishing she'd never given it to him. It was evidence, and evidence was meant to be destroyed.

"I hear you're being indicted," Vivian said. She turned back to him and finished her morning coffee. Clarette's had the best exotic blend from some African county. Who knew they grew coffee beans in Africa, she wondered. The world was truly amazing.

"The Duval bitch wants me," Raul said bitterly. "But that doesn't mean she'll get me."

"No," said Vivian. "I don't suppose she will."

The words sent a chill through Raul. Did Vivian know something about his future whereabouts she wasn't telling him? Had she already found a spot to bury him beneath a blanket of lime? He glanced toward the door, wondering if Leon was lurking nearby with a pistol and a silencer.

"I must go now," Vivian said. "Don't worry, I won't post our little picture from this breakfast, it's only for me. To remember you by, Raul, since we will never meet again."

She stood up. He reached over and placed his hand over hers in a gesture she took as mildly threatening. She did not like being touched, and she did not like being stopped from leaving. She pulled her hand away.

"What do you want, Raul? I don't have any more money for you. I know a half million dollars doesn't go far, but it's all you'll get from me."

"I want assurances, Vivian," he said, regretting having gestured so aggressively toward her.

"Assurances of what?"

"Of, you know . . . "

"Assurance that I won't kill you?" She smiled. What he wanted was such an easy thing to provide. "Don't worry, Raul. I've never killed anyone in my life."

And that was true. Vivian LaGrange had never ended anyone's life, not personally. That's what she had men like Leon for.

She said no more, taking her purse and heading toward the door.

Raul watched her, wondering how close Leon was to the restaurant's entrance. He knew she never strayed far from her bodyguard. Leon was much more than that, but on trips like this he probably stayed in a Mercedes somewhere down the street where he could see Vivian emerge from the restaurant and glide up to the curb.

He was confident she would not have him . . . what was her word? *Removed.* But he couldn't be certain, and he decided, firmly and finally, that Plan B was the only plan left for him, the only one that worked. He would be out of the country by sunset.

He waved at the waiter, who had been standing discreetly in a corner watching them while pretending not to see or hear anything. He wanted another cup of coffee. Why not? Vivian had stuck him with the check, he might as well take his time and enjoy one more delicious cup. Then it was off to the bank and a very special safety deposit box stuffed with hundred dollar bills. He'd always known they would come in handy someday.

CHAPTER Thirty-Four

The man and woman never looked at her. Cecilia had entered the subway train two cars back, then walked forward until she was in the same car, sitting almost directly across from them. They were busy talking. Had they raised their voices just a little more she might have heard them and known what their strategy was, now that they'd spoken to the Ridgley woman. Perhaps they were headed to a police station with whatever information they had, although she doubted it. They had nothing to offer the authorities but the words of a shut-in. The woman seemed the more dangerous of the two; something about her struck Cecilia as especially alert, as if she were accustomed to smelling the air for threat and capable of acting on it. Cecilia saw no sign of a weapon but knew that didn't mean there was none. Knives were easy to conceal; guns, too, if you knew how to hide them.

They got off at the Times Square station, among the city's busiest. It was a hub, with many of the city's subway lines converging into one massive underground gathering. You could go anywhere in the five boroughs from here. It made the station an easy target, and a well-guarded one. Police in SWAT gear, bomb-sniffing dogs, and quite a few undercover cops, all watching the people come and go, the tide of humanity rolling in every few minutes as trains dropped off, picked up, dropped off, picked up and snaked their way back out into the metropolis.

She knew the man's name was Kyle Callahan, Leon told her that. She did not know the woman's name because Leon did not know it. She'd followed them from Callahan's apartment building to the Village where they spoke to the witness, the one they should have silenced (*Leon, oh Leon*, she thought, *Vivian does makes mistakes, I told you so*). Then she followed them back, so close on the train she could almost hear the words Callahan was emphatically whispering, his hands jabbing the air to make points. And now she followed them as they walked from Times Square to 38th Street and west. She wondered where they could be headed as she stayed a half block behind, careful not to draw attention to herself in any way. The woman looked back twice, sensing something was off. Cecilia was an accomplished tail and just kept walking, only slower, so she would not appear to be stopping when the woman looked at her. Nor did she look back; she was just another pedestrian on the sidewalk, maybe going to work late, maybe unemployed.

They crossed Ninth Avenue and headed up another half block. Then, to Cecilia's surprise, they stopped at a large four-story building and went in. It looked like a factory, which is what the Japan TV3 studios had once been. Much of Hell's Kitchen and Chelsea had been industrial a hundred years ago. It was called *Hell's Kitchen* for a reason, and even with its gentrification and its soaring rents, it still felt decrepit. It still had a grittiness to it that made one expect an accompanying stink, which was true enough in the summer months.

Cecilia was perplexed. What was this place? And why would they come here? She kept walking until she was in front of the building. A large sign announced it as Japan TV3. *TV. News.* Vivian LaGrange had an aversion to publicity and had never been on the news, not even when her son was nearly arrested for three capital murders.

She walked into the lobby, acting as if she were a tourist who'd lost her way.

"May I help you?" the man at the front desk asked.

Cecilia looked around her, feigning curiosity. "What is this place?" she asked innocently.

"It's a TV studio. They make Tokyo Pulse here, and a bunch of other stuff. You probably never heard of it. Are you lost?"

"No, no," Cecilia said. "I'm just walking around. Such a fascinating city you have."

The guard thought it was an odd area to be lost in. Most tourists did not wander this far afield.

"Well, unless you have an appointment I can't really let you—"

"No problem," Cecilia said. "No problem at all. Thanks for your time."

She left the studio and the suspicious guard. At least they'd hired someone who cared enough to *be* suspicious. Most were unconcerned with the safety of anyone but themselves. She'd walked past many front desks in her life, it wasn't hard, and she could walk past this one if she had to. Or find another way in.

She headed across the street to a parking lot entrance, took out her phone and dialed.

"Yes?" Leon said on the other end.

Cecilia smiled. Leon tried to sound threatening and to most people he probably did. But not to Cecilia. She knew him too well; very well, in fact. So well she'd had to do a home pregnancy test a year ago when her period was two weeks late. Luckily it had only been a scare and she had not been faced with terminating a pregnancy. Even a woman as hard and unsentimental as Cecilia had her soft spots.

"We have a problem," she said, staring back at the Japan TV3 studios.

"And what would that be?" said Leon.

Cecilia told him about her morning and what she'd seen, about their visit to the Ridgley woman, the ride back on the subway with the man speaking dramatically and the woman—the dangerous one—sensing they were being followed but not sure enough of it to do anything.

"Every problem has a solution," Leon said. He'd lowered his voice, and Cecilia wondered if Vivian was near. Vivian LaGrange—now there was a truly scary woman. The only person who could make Cecelia Ramirez fear for her life. But, as Leon had just said, every problem has a solution.

"Come back," Leon said. "I'll take it from here."

"That's it?" she replied. "I give up my morning to follow them, and that's it?"

"You had other plans?"

"My plans are always to serve, Leon. I just meant . . ."

"I know what you meant. Now go home. That's it for now."

This time there was real threat in his voice and Cecelia wondered if she'd crossed a line. She was known to be flippant and occasionally insubordinate, but surely he wasn't angry with her.

"It's a television station," she said, quickly trying to change the subject. "What if it's not the police they plan on talking to?"

"He works there."

"The Callahan guy?"

"Yes, the Callahan guy. He works at the TV station."

"Interesting."

"Isn't it," said Leon.

"Should I leave town?" she asked.

"Not at all. Just go home Cecilia."

"And do what?"

"Wait."

Leon hung up. Cecilia stared at her phone as if something more would be said, one more word of instruction or reassurance that everything would be fine, but the line was dead. Thinking on it, she wondered if the phone would not be the only dead thing by day's end.

CHAPTER Thirty-Five

Raul had not wanted this and now that he was sitting on his couch across from Vivian LaGrange he had the unsettling feeling he was about to make a mistake. As with many of his decisions in life, he chose to look at it as a wager — he was a gambling man, and this was just one of his higher-stakes bets. He was betting he could take the $500,000 LaGrange was offering him to dismiss the case against her son and not be implicated in any wrong doing. Greed does this to a man. It makes him forget the odds against him. It makes him say yes to the outlandish, when in truth he should run the other way. It was a fairly ridiculous assumption: that he could cut loose a man accused of executing three people and not have the stain of it spill onto his own life. But there was the money, sitting at Vivian's feet in a most stylish briefcase. He wondered if she'd purchased it specifically for this purpose. He could smell them both — the briefcase and the money. He could almost see the hundred dollar bills inside, so green and pristine in all those stacks tied with paper ribbons. What the hell, he decided, it wasn't even the biggest bribe he'd ever taken!

Vivian had also been uncomfortable, but she did not show it in any way. She wasn't worried about being implicated in her son's very bad behavior. She wasn't even concerned about being caught in some bribery scandal with the slick but reptilian Raul Sandoval. She was simply uneasy being seen anywhere in public, with anyone. Vivian had survived in one of the few businesses that can truly be called cutthroat by being fierce, unflinching, and largely unseen. Coming to the Centurion to meet with Manhattan's District Attorney was as chancy for her as it was for Sandoval. She didn't like being exposed, and she sure as hell didn't like being seen with a man her enemies considered a threat. They might think she was there to make a deal, and not the kind that would give her son a chance to leave the country.

"So are we in agreement?" Vivian said. She'd been at the apartment for a half hour and was ready to leave. She'd noticed photographs of Gloria Sandoval and their two daughters and she

wanted to make sure the missus did not come home while she was bribing her husband. She might get the right idea.

"We are," said Raul. "There will not be a grand jury convened for the terrible incident on Greenwich Street. There's simply not enough solid evidence. The sunglasses that fell out of your son's pocket — oh, wait, that never happened because he wasn't there — mysteriously vanished. These things happen. And the one witness has admitted her confusion and declined to identify anyone."

"You know this because you've reviewed the case personally?"

"Yes, I have."

"It seems everything is in order, then," she said, sliding the briefcase toward him.

All odors are particulate. Raul decided that was why he could smell significant amounts of cash — all those money-particles wafting into the air. He stood, walked to the briefcase and picked it up.

"I'll just put this away," he said. He hurried into the bedroom. A moment later he returned without the briefcase. "Let me walk you out, Ms. LaGrange."

"V is fine," she said, smiling. Only people who knew who she was and feared her for it called her that. Telling him amused her.

A minute later they were downstairs, exiting the ornate elevator and walking out of the apartment building. He escorted her past the guard station and out the front entrance where Leon was waiting in a black Escalade.

That's when he saw them: two teenage girls with the worst timing imaginable. They smiled facing away from Raul and Vivian, snapping pictures of themselves with the Centurion behind them.

Raul froze. This was not good.

"What's wrong?" Vivian said. She felt his hand on her arm, pulling her suddenly to the side.

"I can't be seen with you," he said. "That's what's wrong."

"Well, your guard just saw us, and the doorman."

"They don't count. They don't say what they see and they don't pay it any mind. They're like furniture."

"I bet you don't tell them that," she said. She glanced out and saw the girls talking.

"I have a favor," Raul said.

"Does that mean I get my money back?" she replied.

"I'm very serious, Vivian. I cannot have photographs of us out there. Those two girls just took our picture. At least once, probably two or three times."

Vivian thought a moment. "I think you're overreacting, Mr. Sandoval, but I can take care of this if you'd like."

"And how would you do that?"

"I'd take possession of the phone, that's how," Vivian said. "Or, rather, someone would take possession of it for me. I never do anything people say I do, you understand?"

"Completely."

"You would like that, then? We can call this one a favor, or perhaps a bonus."

"I would like that very much," Raul said. "And I would like to know it's been done."

"Don't worry," Vivian said as Leon pulled the Escalade into the drive. "I'll give you the phone as proof."

It was a promise that froze his blood. It was also a promise that Vivian kept, resulting in the inadvertent death of Corrine Copley and the ruin of her father, a promise that, once kept, could never be gone back upon.

CHAPTER Thirty-Six

Kyle and Linda were sitting in Lenny-san's office with Imogene. Leonard Baumstein sat behind the desk in front of them, worrying a paper clip between his right thumb and index finger. Kyle's idea was too big, too explosive, to run without approval. They needed the boss's sign-off, and Kyle knew from experience that was not easy to get. Imogene had pitched dozens of stories to Lenny over the years that he'd rejected, and taking on the Manhattan District Attorney at the height of his infamy was not something to be done on speculation. Still, Kyle could tell he had Lenny's interest. The man had gone through three papers clips listening to him make the case for running the story so soon. The consequences would be immense either way: if they were right, it would be the kind of once-in-a-lifetime feature that sent them all to the top of the heap and put Emmys on their bookshelves; if they were wrong, their careers would be finished by Monday

"Let me get this straight," Leonard said. "You have a witness in the Village who can connect Raul Sandoval to the LaGrange woman."

"To her lieutenant," Kyle said. "A guy named Leon Carter. She changed her testimony after Leon pressured her into forgetting what she'd seen."

"Right, right," Imogene said. She was clearly excited by the story. She'd wanted to climb the next wrung of the career ladder at Japan TV3 but knew there was no next wrung: Leonard Baumstein was standing on it. She would need something to take her out of here altogether, a story big enough to get her an offer from one of the networks, or maybe NYNow, the 24/7 New York City-only channel that fed the Big Three so many of their reporters. To them NYNow was a stepping stone, but for someone like Imogene, fifty-three years old and viewed not long ago as a has-been, a high-profile slot at the popular channel would be a crowning achievement.

She'd always wanted to anchor. Hell, she'd settle for City Reporter with them, and she would take Kyle with her. But first she had to have a coup de grâce, a story so big it could not be ignored. And, it went without saying, exclusive.

"The crime boss's right hand tells the witness to change her story," Imogene continued. "The crime boss's son gets cut loose from a triple homicide charge, *and* the witness sees the lead detective on the Corinne Copley murder talking to the right hand. She connects the dots and never leaves her apartment again."

"We're not sure she connected the dots," Linda said. She'd been watching it all with fascination. The workings of a news room were completely foreign to her. She'd known reporters in her life, and had been interviewed quite a few times during her tenure with the New Hope Police Force, but she had no idea how stories were pitched and decided. She also wasn't sure they had enough to run with, but she would leave that up to the professionals. "We only know she made the connection between the killings downstairs, Leon Carter and Detective Dietz. She doesn't know there's any connection between them and Corinne Copley."

"But I do," Kyle said. He'd been running on adrenaline for the past two hours. He was certain Corinne Copley died for the photographs she'd taken in front of the Centurion, photos that showed Raul Sandoval with someone. Who would that someone be? Leon Carter? Detective Dietz?

"So what's the story?" Lenny said. "What are we saying in front of eight million New Yorkers? Probably the world if this blows up the way I expect it will."

"We're saying Raul Sandoval has been connected—"

"By a source close to the investigation," Imogene said, finishing the thought.

"What investigation?" asked Lenny.

"*Our* investigation," Imogene responded, annoyed by Lenny's hesitation. "Any investigation we want it to be. I can't say it's from an anonymous source. We have to give it more credence than that. So let's go with, 'A source close to the investigation into the brutal murders in Greenwich Village' — scratch that, 'the brutal *drug-related* murders in Greenwich Village three years ago has revealed a close connection between Manhattan District Attorney Raul Sandoval and Vivian LaGrange, the mother of the man thought at the time to be responsible for the killings." Then, to Kyle, "You should be writing this down. It's our copy."

"I'll remember," said Kyle, not wanting to interrupt her train of thought.

"A witness has come forward," Imogene continued, "connecting the infamous criminal overlord with the most powerful law enforcement officer in the city."

"The Queens D.A. won't appreciate that," Lenny said. "Or the Bronx D.A., or . . ."

"We're looking at a national story," Imogene said. "And as far as Raul Sandoval is concerned, he is the most powerful law enforcement officer in New York City. The Big Fish. The one we're going to fry."

"I thought this was a TV show in Japan," Linda said.

Imogene looked at Lenny. They both knew they were sitting on a powder keg and about to light the fuse.

"It will go out as breaking," Lenny said. "All news is global now, if it's big enough. We break the story on Japan TV3 — and I don't mean Tokyo Pulse, Imogene's baby. I mean their main news channel."

"Seriously?" said Imogene. She hadn't concerned herself with the logistics, only with getting the story down.

"I'll call the boys in Tokyo as soon as we're finished here," Lenny said. "They've been wanting to expand in America. I think I know just the man to lead that."

He was referring to himself and Imogene knew it. She did not know if his plans included her. At the same time, she hoped they didn't. She was ready to jump ship and opportunity was pounding on the door at that very moment.

"So what's our follow up?" Kyle asked. He knew once they went live with the story the full weight of the New York media would bear down on them, as well as the full weight of Raul Sandoval's attorneys and possibly the fire power of one Vivian LaGrange. They might need protection. His mind was swirling ever-faster as the possible repercussions played in his imagination.

"We get the witness to go public," Imogene said. "We add an angle about corruption in the NYPD . . ."

"It's just one dirty cop," Linda said. As a retired officer she was alarmed they were suddenly implicating the entire police force of the largest city in the country.

"I throw the bombs," Imogene said. "I can't be responsible for the shrapnel."

"Linda's right," Kyle said, fearful Imogene would sabotage the whole thing with her own ambitions. "For now. And we're not there yet, anyway."

"Not there yet?" asked Lenny.

"He's got a point," said Imogene. "This is just the opening salvo. We can layer this for days, spread the story out and see where its tentacles go. Hell, Lenny, we might be looking at a Pulitzer. Call the Times, make a deal."

"First things first," Lenny said. "We get the initial story out, the connection between Sandoval, LaGrange and the murders, and we go from there. Very, very carefully."

Kyle could tell the meeting was over by the silence that came over them as Lenny tossed the last paper clip in the trash can and did not reach for another. He wanted to make phone calls. He wanted to make arrangements. And he wanted them out of his office.

Two minutes later they were clustered at Kyle's cubicle. He was already exhausted from the emotional surge of the past half hour. Were they doing the right thing? He had to believe it. He also had to believe it would work. There was nowhere else to go with the story. The police would only drag their feet and demand some slow, methodical investigation, if they initiated one at all. Louise Ridgley could be dead by then. So, too, might Kyle. They'd exposed themselves and he was sure Vivian LaGrange and Raul Sandoval would hear about it, if they hadn't already.

"Get Stanley on the phone," Imogene said. Stanley was both her cameraman and assistant producer. For her first five years doing Tokyo Pulse she had been a one-woman show, filming herself with a tripod and editing the footage well into the night. But since the Pride Lodge murders, the Pride Gallery killings, and the huge Pride Killer story, she'd graduated to having a team consisting of Stanley and Kyle.

"Where are you going to shoot?" Kyle asked, his hand already on the phone.

"In front of the D.A's office, where else?" Imogene said. Her voice was lower now, emotionless. Her expression was severe: she knew what she was about to do would either succeed spectacularly or destroy her. Finally, in these moments before the biggest story of her career, it was all or nothing.

"Call him," she said. "Have him meet me at the van."

Kyle dialed Stanley's number.

"Oh, and Kyle, you're going with me."

He stopped dialing.

"It's time you learned how to produce," Imogene said. "Since you'll be getting a credit on this one."

Kyle went back to dialing the cameraman's cell phone. His hand was shaking.

CHAPTER Thirty-Seven

The end of the week was usually busy for Raul. He had various legal issues to consider, a calendar to review for the following week, cancellations, and unexpected appointments. He would normally be engrossed in work from the time he woke up at 4:00 a.m. until the time he met Gloria for dinner — they always ate out on Fridays. It was the most expensive day of the week for him. But today was different. This Friday was not like any other he had experienced or ever would: he would be leaving New York City by nightfall, on a plane to Spain. He'd not decided where he would go from there, or what identity he would assume. He did not doubt Eleanor Duvall would attempt to find him and drag him back in handcuffs. An escape might well mean becoming someone else. Fortunately he had the connections to make that happen, but not before he left the country. There was no time to call in the many favors owed him by the sort of people who can manufacture new identities. It would have to wait until he was in a hotel room in Barcelona with a small suitcase filled with cash — not the kind you checked at curbside.

He was too energized to be sad. He would miss his daughters Michaela and Lorraine, but not their mother. She had cost him nearly as much money as he was taking out of the country with him, possibly several times that. He would find a way to contact the girls. They would be fine, he told himself. Their college was paid for. He'd set up trusts for each of them just in case of such an event. They would do well without him, and they would be spared the humiliation of seeing their father dragged through the mud, paraded like some trophy by the bitch Duvall.

He had his plane ticket. He had his small suitcase of clothes and his matching suitcase of cash — nearly $1M in crisp, bundled stacks. He had his passport, the one they would confiscate if he stayed much longer. He had his plans. It was just a matter of leaving soon and getting a taxi to the airport.

He was looking at the framed pictures of his daughters one last time, his gaze lingering on them—how much Michaela looked like his mother, how homely Lorraine was, so beautifully, achingly homely—when his assistant Donna knocked on the door. It was an urgent knock, a knock he'd only heard in the most pressing situations. He glanced at the two suitcases under his desk.

"Yes, Donna?" he said.

She knocked again, then entered. She had been Raul's secretary for ten years, before his spectacular climb to the District Attorney's office and then to its epicenter.

"Raul," she said. Her face was ashen, a frown embedded on her lips.

"I'm not feeling patient today," he said. "I have an appointment. What brings you barging into my office? Has the mayor died? I'd think that would make you smile."

"No," she said. "No one's died. But there's a camera crew outside."

"Outside?"

"On the sidewalk. A woman and a camera man, and she's . . . saying things."

Raul felt his stomach drop into his shoes. He suddenly had the need to evacuate his bowels. Something was going wrong, and going wrong right then.

He got up and crossed to the window. He could see the street below, the front entrance to the D.A.'s office. Sure enough, four floors down was a small woman, made even smaller by the distance, talking into a microphone. Six feet in front of her was a man holding a camera. Off to the side he saw another man with a notepad, and a tall woman.

"What are they saying?" Raul said, his voice low.

"Turn on the TV and listen," Donna said. "It's running live on NYNow."

Lenny-san had made calls after Imogene, Kyle and Linda left his office. This was very big news, and an enormous risk. He was gambling his career on this story being right, even if the details were sketchy now. His bosses in Tokyo had been very interested in the story. They'd also known this was much bigger than Tokyo Pulse, bigger than Japan TV3 itself, and they needed a partner. They were not in a position to break a story this explosive on an obscure cable channel in New York, so after getting the green light from them, Lenny called his old friend Janet Merchant at NYNow. Yes, it was big enough for a major network, but wouldn't it be amazing for them both to break the story instead? NYNow's ratings would go through the roof. They would have exclusive credits, maybe exclusive interviews, but they had to act now.

Imogene, Kyle, Linda and cameraman Stanley were at the District Attorney's office twenty minutes later, set up by the front entrance. Imogene was broadcasting live, the story was catching fire:

. . . A source close to the investigation of the grisly triple homicide on Greenwich Street has told me there's a connection between the unindicted suspect Jordan LaGrange, said to now be living in Bermuda, and Manhattan's own District Attorney Raul Sandoval. According to this source, that connection is LaGrange's mother Vivian, believed by many to run New York City's drug trade. Tokyo Pulse, working with NYNow, has obtained evidence of this link and will be updating you regularly and exclusively throughout the day . . .

Kyle wanted to vomit. There was no evidence, only a frightened witness they'd just put in jeopardy, and a great deal of speculation. He was wondering what he'd done and what the repercussions would be when Raul Sandoval himself came barreling through the main entrance to the D.A.'s office.

"You lying bitch!" he said, rushing toward Imogene.

It was Linda Sikorsky who stepped in front of the diminutive reporter to block Sandoval's path.

"Who the fuck are you?" he said to her.

"I'm a police officer," she said, leaving out the "retired."

He froze, then looked quickly around. Were there other police here? Was Eleanor Duvall waiting around a corner to arrest him? *For what?* They had no proof—not of his bribery, not of his arrangement with Vivian LaGrange, and certainly not of his involvement with the Corinne Copley murder.

Or is Vivian behind this, he wondered. Is that why she suddenly wanted the phone back, to protect herself while she whispered in some two-bit reporter's ear and sent the hounds after him. *Well, well, that won't last long,* he thought. *We'll see who takes down whom.*

"There's nothing to these lies," he said to Imogene, speaking past Linda who had taken a firm stand between them. "Nothing but one huge fucking lawsuit. You'll be waiting tables when this is over."

Imogene smiled at him. "I've waited them before," she said. "Now, if you'll excuse us, we have a story to edit."

She nodded at Stanley. A moment later the four of them were walking away, back to the Japan TV3 van parked around the corner.

Kyle was feeling sicker by the minute. Chasing down murderers had been less harrowing than chasing down one of the most powerful men in New York City. The others could have killed him; this one could leave him alive and ruined.

"I hope we did the right thing," he said, thinking of Skate, knowing if this led where he believed it did, they had made the right decision.

"Of course we did," Imogene said, leading them to the van. "People love watching the mighty fall, and we have just sent Raul Sandoval teetering toward the edge."

Yes, we have, Kyle thought. He knew Eleanor Duvall would see the short breaking news they'd just blasted out into the world, if she hadn't seen it already. Whatever blood from Raul Sandoval had flavored the water for her would now be a torrent. Duvall, the Great White, and her many little sharks would come in for the kill.

Kyle stopped short of the van.

"Are you all right?" Linda asked.

"I will be," he said, then he knelt down and puked.

CHAPTER Thirty-Eight

By that evening Imogene's explosive news report was in heavy rotation and spreading quickly. The involvement of Vivian LaGrange, and the verification "from a source close to the investigation" that she had worked with, or rather hired, Raul Sandoval, added a salaciousness that made it ripe to go viral. It had everything: politics, murder, bribery, dead bodies, and a baby left to stare silently at its mother's corpse. The headlines wrote themselves.

The sharks had come in for the kill and reporters from every channel were scrambling to catch up with the story Imogene Landis first put a match to; it was only a matter of days—hours?—before every rock was overturned by some intrepid journalist looking for victims to interview and people to plead for "closure."

Robin Dietz was fucked and he knew it. He'd been involved in both cases. He'd been the lead detective in the Corinne Copley murder, making sure the investigation went in any direction but the right one. He'd been party to the miraculous freeing of Jordan LaGrange, telling Leon Carter who the witness was and how easily she could be persuaded to forget what she'd seen. And he'd given Skate Copley copies of reports and inside information that would, by itself, cost him his job, his retirement, and his pension.

He sat on his couch watching the report run again. The volume was down; he did not want to hear the woman's voice anymore, almost chipper as she told the world that Raul Sandoval had been in league with the city's biggest, baddest crime boss to get her son off the hook for assassinating three people in a minor drug dispute. He knew it would not be long before his name came up. It made him glad he was divorced, glad he had no children, glad there was no one in the world who would miss him except his mother and the bartenders at

Mackey's. The thought made him smile: he was about to become the biggest star Mackey's Star Bar had ever seen.

At least he wouldn't have to pay off his debts. He wouldn't have to ignore letters from Mom sent to a prison address or refuse visits from a son he didn't have and who, if he'd existed, probably wouldn't want to visit his dirty-cop father anyway.

He watched the woman talking silently. *Imogene Landis.* It was a good day for Imogene, oh yes. If no one had ever heard of her before today, they would know her now. Both of them would be famous very soon. At least they had that in common.

He placed the barrel of his service revolver in his mouth, aiming upward to the top of his skull, and pulled the trigger.

CHAPTER Thirty-Nine

Vivian had seen the news reports several times. The breaking story with that small, strange woman, and the stories that followed it as the other news channels tried to match her. They couldn't, at least not yet. But they would. She sighed. She was unperturbed for the most part; a woman like Vivian did not survive this long without being able to stay calm in the severest of storms, and this one looked bad. She would have to call Jordan and convince him to move again, this time to a country that did not have an extradition treaty with the United States. She might join him there. Nothing really prevented her from running her business offshore, it would just make it harder for her and easier for those who would like to see her retire, alive or dead.

"Leon," she called out. He'd been hovering all day, stepping out on the balcony to smoke every half hour. He was nervous. He was almost as well known as Vivian, at least by everyone who did business with her, and he would not likely escape the fallout from this, certainly not once his role in the witness tampering was known.

"Just a moment, Boss," he called out from the bathroom. He'd gone in there several times, too, more than usual, and Vivian wondered if he was on his phone whispering to some travel agent.

"We need to make arrangements," she called out, wanting his response now, not when it was convenient for him. She had taken very good care of Leon over the years, and in return she expected him to jump as far and high as she needed him to, when she needed him to.

"I have, Boss," he said. The sound of his voice was so close it startled her. *Damn, he's good at his job*, she thought. She hadn't heard him come up behind her, and so quickly.

She started to turn toward him, to give him orders and set her plans in motion.

He pressed the silencer against her head — such pretty hair, so little gray — and sent a slug careening through and around Vivian LaGrange's brain.

Finally.

"It's done," he said into his cell phone. He felt badly, but not too. He knew — and he believed Vivian knew, too — it would come to this eventually.

"Are you okay?" Cecilia said, her voice soothing over the phone.

"I'm fine," he said. "I need to leave. I need to call Salazar. He owes me for this. And he's hiring. Now pack for Toronto, we're going on a long vacation."

"I love you so much, Leon. Leon the Lion."

"I love you too, Poodle."

Leon Carter clicked off the call and slipped the phone into his jacket pocket. He would have to throw the jacket away — backsplash from Vivian's head wound had dotted it with spots of blood. He would probably throw the phone away, too, and say it was lost if anyone asked. They would know he'd been in the building when Vivian was killed once they got the cell tower data, but he lived downstairs, of course he was here.

"Sorry, Boss," he said to Vivian's corpse, now slumped forward on her couch. "It's just business."

Leon Carter left Vivian LaGrange's apartment, never to return. It had been a good, long run, and the risks had been matched by the perks. Leon would miss them, but he saw life as a series of opportunities. He had taken one with the woman on the couch in front of him, not so pretty now, and he would take a new one with Pedro Salazar.

Nobody lives forever. Leon knew that. He knew the day would come when someone, maybe even his beloved Cecilia, his *Poodle*, stepped up behind him and told him it was time to go, just like that.

Leon took a deep breath, slipped his gun into his pocket next to the phone, both of which would be rusting at the bottom of the Hudson River within the hour, and let himself out of the apartment.

CHAPTER Forty

It wasn't exactly a party at the 38-Nine Deli, but everyone was there: Kyle, Linda, Niz, his wife Meriem, and the guest of honor in this sad drama—Skate Copley. Kyle had told Imogene there was something he had to do after they got back to the Japan TV3 studios. She'd balked at first, wanting him with her to follow up on what had become a fast breaking story, until she saw his look of determination and thought better of resisting. He'd brought this to her, after all, a priceless gift for any reporter's career.

"Go, then, and come back in the morning," she'd said. "It's been a hell of a day for you, Kyle. And we have things to talk about."

"Things?" he'd said. Linda was standing next to him at his cubicle. She casually walked away, giving them as much privacy as they could get in an open seating arrangement.

"I've already heard from NYNow," Imogene said, glancing toward Lenny-san's office. "They want me for special assignments."

Kyle stared at her. He'd known this was coming but he'd never thought it would be this sudden.

"Don't worry," Imogene said. "Where I go, you go. I'm not leaving you, Kyle. I'm taking you with me!"

"Does Lenny know?" Kyle asked.

"Of course. Who do you think our producer's going to be?"

Holy shit, thought Kyle. This was big news, and an enormous change. NYNow wasn't quite the Big Time, but it was bigger than Tokyo Pulse, bigger than Japan TV3. A niche market is huge when the market is New York City.

"I thought Lenny wanted to run Japan TV3's national expansion?"

"He thought better of it after two vodka rocks and a reality check. It's an administrative position with them, boring, and all roads lead to Tokyo. Lenny's like me, really, he loves the story, the hunt. He'll make less money this way, but not by much, and he'll be a hundred times happier. *We'll* be happier.

We'll be happier. Kyle didn't know if she meant himself and Imogene, or the three of them, or, as he'd sometimes suspected (and hoped), Lenny and Imogene as a possible couple. They'd both been alone as long as he'd known them. Wouldn't it be something if they discovered a passion for more than chasing stories together?

"Now go," Imogene said. "We'll talk tomorrow. And rest up tonight, you're going to need it. We all are."

Kyle hugged her then. He'd been with her for nearly eight years. And he was ready for something different. How much better could it be than to make that change with Imogene and Lenny?

Linda, too, said her goodbyes. She was planning to head back to New Jersey in the morning. There'd been enough excitement the last few days to last quite some time, and besides, Kirsten was getting impatient. She'd told Linda on their call that morning that she liked living in the woods well enough, but not alone. There were bats and spiders and snakes and all kinds of insect noises that got deafening at night. Linda was to return as soon as possible — please.

They left the studios and made the short walk to the 38-Nine Deli. Kyle had been surprised to see Niz and his wife there, then realized why they'd gathered: to watch Imogene's news report now running on every news channel in the city, and to see Raul Sandoval being arrested at the airport.

"Oh my God," Kyle said, standing at the cash register with his back turned to Skate as they watched the small television behind the counter.

Raul had attempted to pursue his Plan B, managing to slip out of the D.A.'s office with two suitcases, one filled with cash. He'd even made it to the gate for his Delta flight to Barcelona. But he had not boarded the plane. Two plainclothes policemen had stopped him and escorted him out of the airport, all the way to justice, should it prevail.

"Dietz killed himself," Skate said.

"What?" said Kyle, startled.

"They found his body in his apartment. Shot himself. They didn't say there was a connection, but I'm guessing there must be. You think he was involved in Corinne's murder?"

Kyle didn't have an answer. So many assumptions had been made to get this story out, so many risks taken. Dietz was surely involved in the deal to let Jordan LaGrange go, but how it was connected to Corinne's death was still unclear, if it was connected at all.

"What about Vivian LaGrange?" Linda asked. Sandoval's great crime was done at LaGrange's request, in exchange for LaGrange's money.

"Dead," said Skate. "It's been a big day for news. They're falling all over themselves to tell the story. Sandoval goes down, Dietz and LaGrange are dead. But nothing about Corinne. Not a word."

Kyle turned and looked at Skate. He was as thin and drawn as ever, but something seemed less haggard, less troubled.

"Don't worry," Kyle said. "There will be. Imogene will see to that."

"Who's Imogene?" said Skate. Then, realizing she was the woman who'd done the reporting, he said, "Oh, yes, of course. If you say so . . ."

"I say so," Kyle said. "Can we talk a moment?"

Skate looked at Niz for permission to leave his station behind the deli counter. Niz nodded, and Skate came around front. He and Kyle walked out onto the sidewalk.

"How are you doing?" Kyle said. "Really doing."

Skate thought a long moment. He started to speak, then stopped, then started again.

"I'm . . . whatever I am, Kyle. Still fucked. Still alone. Still without my daughter. Does this arrest make me feel better, and the death of Dietz? It will if something comes of it, some reason."

"It will," said Kyle. "I don't know how yet, but I know it will. Corinne wasn't killed by some street thug looking for a phone to sell for his next bag of meth or crack or whatever he was hooked on. She was killed for a photograph."

"A photograph?" Skate said, shocked.

"Yes. A photograph. And Raul Sandoval was in it. Probably with Vivian LaGrange. He couldn't be seen with New York City's biggest criminal coming out of his apartment building. I think he just wanted the camera, though. I don't think Corrine was supposed to die for it." All speculation, but so much of it had been.

"That doesn't make it any better," Skate said. "She's still gone and she's never coming back."

"No, she's not," said Kyle. "But I'll tell you what. She finally spoke."

Speak to me, Baby, just speak to me. The words had haunted Skate Copley's every waking moment for three years. He did not expect it to stop now, but to not be quite so *distressing*. Corinne had spoken to them, and the time had come to let go, however slightly. He would have to get back to living now, back to facing a life without his singular obsession. A trial would help, even if Sandoval was the only one left to hold accountable. He would be able to tell the story, to admit what happened that horrible, awful, unforgettable day. Having the truth come out would help. And knowing he had never given up would help most of all.

Kyle turned to Skate and put his arms around him. They hugged each other on Ninth Avenue, appearing to anyone passing as two men saying goodbye for the evening. Instead, they were two men saying hello to lives about to change.

CHAPTER Forty-One

Goodbyes were often sad. Sometimes only one person knew it was final, adding a burden of secrecy to the parting. Other times, like tonight, both knew they would likely not see each other again and the words took on an added melancholy.

It had been two weeks since Kyle sat in Peter Benoit's office. As he looked around he reflected that, while nothing had changed—the statue of Chopin was still there, the photographs, the desk—everything had changed. Kyle had caught another killer, or at least the people responsible for the killing. He was no longer depressed. The nightmares had stopped.

"I'm very happy for you," Peter said. He was not given to showing emotion; it didn't suit his profession. But even a therapist had feelings, and Kyle knew Peter had a place in his heart for him. They might be friends under different circumstances. "When does the new job start?"

Kyle smiled. As expected, Imogene had been offered and had accepted a position as a field reporter for NYNow. And not just any field reporter, but a star, a major attraction. Lenny-san, too, had been offered a job as a senior producer. (He had insisted on the "senior" in his title, and he would be dropping the "-san" from his name now that Japanese was not his bosses' first language.) Kyle would continue as Imogene's assistant, but more: he would be a production assistant as well, credited on screen. He anticipated a move to producer within a couple years. It gave him a sense of renewal, *renaissance*, for the third act of his life.

"We're moving to the NYNow offices on Tuesday," Kyle said. "After the obligatory cake and congratulations on Monday. I haven't see them yet but I'm told they're bigger and nicer, in Chelsea. I'll still be able to walk to work."

"This is all good news for you, Kyle," Peter said. He was not writing anything down; taking notes was not his style, and he usually made them after his clients left, although he kept a notepad handy in case something came up in the conversation he needed to flag. "Is Danny happy with all this?"

"I thought 'happy' wasn't a word therapists used," said Kyle.

"Where did you get that idea?"

"I don't know, I just thought . . . it gets so real in here. 'Happy' seems like something for a greeting card, not an analyst's couch."

"So it's a word you wouldn't use. But I would! I want you to be happy. Mostly I'm just glad you're not having nightmares anymore."

"No, no more nightmares. And to answer your question, yes, Danny is happy. He was worried. He still is, but not so much."

The news they'd broken had become a gathering storm the past two weeks. Raul Sandoval was out on bail—he'd never been *in*, actually, but he had stepped down as Manhattan's District Attorney and hired the best, most expensive defense lawyer a hundred thousand dirty dollars could retain. The legal fees just might wipe out the fortune he'd made in bribes.

Robin Dietz was now several pages in an ongoing investigation and not much more. His name had already been destroyed with stories of a bad cop, a chronic gambler and a participant in an elaborate set of circumstances that included the murder of a teenage girl on 37th Street. Vivian LaGrange was gone, too, but not easily forgotten. Her empire existed in the shadows, and the power struggles that followed her death were waged unseen by the public, except for several murders that could not yet be attributed to the maneuverings of aspiring crime lords. Leon Carter had emerged unscathed and was somewhere in Canada with his new bride. Had Kyle been privy to the gangland rumor mill, he would know that everyone assumed Leon had ended Vivian's career with a bullet to her head, but proving it was another thing.

"I've gotten a lot out of seeing you the last six months," Kyle said.

"I'm glad to hear that," Peter replied. He glanced at the desk clock, and Kyle could tell it was different this time: Peter wasn't looking to see if their time was up, but because he hoped it wasn't. "You know I'm always here, Kyle. If you need to talk."

"I know that, and I've got you on speed dial."

Peter glanced at the clock again. "Well," he said, easing forward in his chair.

"Well," said Kyle. He reached for his backpack on the floor and opened it. "By the way," he said. "I want to take your picture."

Peter smiled as Kyle took out his camera, the one that had been sitting on a shelf gathering dust since Diedrich Keller's death. "Does this mean what I think it means?" he said.

"Yes, it does," replied Kyle. "I'm a photographer again. Sort of, if the mood strikes me. But it's better than the mood never striking me!"

Kyle took the lens cap off his Nikon D3100. It has been his favorite camera, the one he'd used to take almost all his photographs, although now a good smartphone would do just as well. Technology had come so far.

He paused a moment, frowning.

"What are you thinking?" Peter asked.

"Oh, about photographs and cell phones," Kyle said, remembering Corinne Copley. Her father Skate still worked at the 38-Nine Deli and probably would for some time. A man in such a state of devastation does not rebuild his life in two weeks. It would take awhile, but Skate was not so haunted now, not so unable to live.

"So," said Kyle, "just sit back and look like a gentle, all-knowing therapist."

Peter laughed. "I don't know what one of those looks like."

"So pretend. And don't smile. It looks posed. As a matter of fact, look out the window, as if I'm not here. Good, good. And . . . snap."

Kyle took Peter Benoit's picture. Then he shot another, and another, for good measure. He felt himself wanting to keep clicking the shutter, to stay forever in this safe little room with this kind man who had helped him through his darkest hours. But that was make-believe; that was not life. Life had beginnings, middles and ends. And now, as he put his camera back into his backpack, he knew it was time for an ending.

They both stood up, and finally, after all the words they'd shared and the minutes they had passed together, embraced.

About the Author

Writing is the one thing I've done consistently all my life, whether it was being expressed in short fiction, long fiction, poetry, prose, plays, or children's television scripts. It is the one thing I've always felt compelled to do. Day jobs come and go, but the keyboard is forever. One day, hopefully far in the future, they'll find me dead with my head on the space bar, having passed on to the Great Word Processor in the Sky doing what I loved most to do.

Thanks to anyone and everyone who has spent some time with Kyle and the gang. I hope you'll take another ride on the mystery train, meet a new traveler or two, and keep me getting up before the sun to bring you more.

As for my personal life, I live in New York City with my husband Frank Murray and our dwindling family of cats. We have a house in the rural New Jersey countryside where we plan to move permanently someday ... maybe.

Mark McNease